RED DIE

ROGER NORMAN

THE SUNDIAL PRESS

RED DIE

First published in a hardback edition by The Sundial Press in 2008

This edition published by The Sundial Press in 2012

THE SUNDIAL PRESS
Sundial House
The Sheeplands, Sherborne, Dorset DT9 4BS

www.sundialpress.co.uk

Front cover image: © Alan Baker

Cover Design: Frank Kibblewhite

ISBN 978-1-908274-20-5

CONTENTS

The Ruins of Time build Mansions in Eternity.

William Blake

For Sibel

Chapter One

The Soldier's Return

In November 1917, Lt-Gen. Sir Launcelot Kiggell paid his first visit to the fighting zone. As his staff car lurched through the swampland and neared the battleground he became more and more agitated. Finally he burst into tears and muttered, 'Good God, did we really send men to fight in that?' The man beside him, who had been through the campaign, replied tonelessly, 'It's worse further up.'

(Leon Wolff)

JACK YEOMAN drew the others as a spinning die stirs invisible motes from the surrounding air. There was the captain, and Bill Bate, and the priest. Maggie Fox was drawn in because of him, and it was through him that Cockler got involved. These made up the six, the number of faces on the dice that he carried in his pocket.

At the storming of Maudremont, called by French troops Mont-maudit, the accursed hill, a townful of British soldiers died in a few hours after they were ordered to advance shoulder to shoulder towards the enemy lines carrying sixty-six pounds of assorted military clutter, gasmask and wire cutters and entrenching tools, blanket and water-proof cape and cap comforter, first aid dressings and rations of bully beef and biscuits, not forgetting the pullthrough and oil. As well as the rifle and its two-foot steel bayonet, there were three stick grenades, a belt of ammunition and a water-bottle, spats, leggings, brasses and that coarse dirtgreen shirt, and this is what most of them would die

1

with or die under or if the blast was enough die without. They had with them their paybook too, for every man jack of His Majesty's Forces was entitled to the sum of three bob a week. When they topped the trenches, they were ordered to walk, not run. It is said that some of the German machine gunners eyeing them over the parapets of their trenches were too astonished to open fire, disbelieving that the men who were coming against them should present a target so perfectly set up. One of them commented that it was not unlike shooting tin ducks at a fair, but hold on, it couldn't have been much like that because the tin ducks make it harder by moving across your line of fire, while these lads were coming straight at you. Besides, you had a Messerschmitt machine gun which fired half a belt of slugs in the time it takes to say it, and if only a few rounds found their mark, you'd still have been killing more people in five minutes than there are tin ducks at a fair. No, not much like, because these young soldiers were going down with holes in their heads and bits and pieces of their bodies blown away. Jack Yeoman was one of those to form a search party that night to reclaim the bodies and when they came back the sergeant had written in the report that mainly small fragments were recovered.

Later that night he got a lift away from the lines on a troop carrier with the wounded, and he didn't answer any question that was put to him, so they thought he was shell-shocked or deaf, which common enough. He spoke hardly a word even though he went through two roadblocks and queued up past a checkpoint to board the ship to cross the channel. Here an officer gave him a yellow chit but he threw it to the waves as they crossed. Two lean Scots with a few weeks of beard had come up alongside him near the coast and urged him to join a band of runaways who were living wild in the woods, and this time he stopped and got out the dice and threw them before passing on. But the dice said Circle One which meant to him go on home and that's what he did.

He thought hardly more than he spoke. He kept his mind empty, a thing not hard to do because so many things had been blown out of it. Mostly he watched the road or the verge by the road, and there studied the forms of leaves, and the curve of the grass stems and the small mud sculptures where feet or hooves had passed. Sometimes among the grasses there were dragonflies like overloaded biplanes, and beetles like black tanks and ants hurrying along trenches, and occasionally scarlet ladybirds with one spot or two spots, like emblems of rank or squadron. When he was unsure of the way, he asked the dice to decide, and after a quick glance at what they showed, he would know which road to take. There was one white die and one red one, and the faces of the white die ran from one to six in the usual fashion, but on the red die were six symbols that belonged neither to the Tarot nor to the Torah nor to any known text or rite, at least not in that form and combination. Tower, circle, cross, pillar, sword and skull, they said. When he threw the dice, he would read Tower Three or Pillar Five and set off without hesitation down one road or the other or across the fields instead. His path led him north and then west before finally it took him homewards. Much of the time he was uncertain, of where he was and where he was going and why a part of his mind remained stubbornly behind him in the troglodyte world he had left.

At last, he came into Dorset at Shaftesbury and walked down out of the town by Love Lane to the lower church and its splitflint walls and its clock that didn't work, and out onto the Todber moorland that the gypsies took for their own almost, although this day their wagons weren't there nor their sharp-faced dogs and dappled horses. Next Alton Pancras, settled among the hedges and clays. A dark cloud passed in front of the sun, with its leading fringe elongating like weed in the sea, and these sombre fingers reaching forward across the sky brought back the war all at once so that he walked oblivious by Maid's Hole and Ram's Hill and only came awake again as he entered Manston. Only came really alive once more as he trod the bridge over Manston brook and saw the bruised-grassgreen waters boiling back from under the bridge. The spinney with the unruly holly, and the oaks that the ivy was riotously throttling, and the jackdaws busy over the church,   lolling and flipping, talking harshly to each other and to the world at large.

And here was home, bigger than it need be, as if the house might have had pretensions of grandeur had it not also been a little ugly, and greyly rectangular. An unsmiling house, white casements on a dull grey stone without warmth or fancy, but still home, with chaffinches that nested in the limes and wrens living out whole lives in the yew hedges, and these were what his mother had liked best when she was alive. She never threw away a crumb that might feed them. Next to the house, the river swung by at a trot. You could toss a stone over its breadth, and for half the year the reed banks nearly choked it, but it held good chub for all that and perch up to a pound, and the way the smell of it got sucked up by the air of the yard and spilled over into the fields – this smell of eel and dabchick's feet and riverbank mud, it

4

wasn't what you'd choose for a picnic but it got inside you and even got inside the names of things. Marnhull, Stourton, Sturminster, they all smelled of river, and how could it have been otherwise?

He stood at the side of the house, looking at the river, watching the reeds pushing forward in the current then jerking upright again, and became aware of someone moving in the room behind him. He ducked out of sight and peered through the glass. It was his brother Charles, cleaning his shotgun. There was no lamp lit inside the room, for it was only mid-afternoon, but Jack could see him well enough. He could even see that his hair had gone a little grey at the temples. He could see that everything about him was as neat as ever it was: the line of his hair, the crisp white of his collar, his fingernails. Well, he couldn't see his fingernails but he knew they'd be neatly trimmed and no dirt under. As he stood away from the window, he looked at his own nails, which hadn't been cut for a month nor scrubbed either, and he saw on him the hands of a fighting man, when all the time he'd had a half-suspicion that he was still a boy.

This elaborate care of a weapon for killing birdies! The brass-jointed cleaning rods, the miniature canister of gun oil, the careful disassembly of stock and breech and barrel, the neat compartments of the leather gun-case, lined with green baize like the cloth of a billiard table. The trappings of a gentleman's sport. There had been a time when Jack had loved the smell of that gun oil, but not anymore. He moved quietly from the window and went into the farmyard, past the midden and the sheds. The door of one of the sheds was ajar and through the darkened opening something gleamed faintly, and he approached it slowly, as one would walk up to an animal that might bite. It was the chrome silencer of the Zenith's exhaust pipe. He squatted on the ground, took out the dice and cast them on the flat paving stone at the entrance to the shed. Then he considered, but not for long.

He circled the house watching for Maggie Fox through the windows. When he saw his brother seated at the desk in the study, he entered the house quietly by the side door. He climbed the back stair to the corridor where his bedroom was, with Maggie's next to it. With only the briefest glance at the photograph by his bed of himself looking serious in his mother's arms when he was five or six, he took off his army denims and stuffed them into his kitbag and stuffed that in turn under his bed. He put on britches and a woollen jersey and from the top drawer of the desk he took out pen and paper and a ten shilling note hidden at the back. He went into Maggie's room and wrote a message which he put on her pillow. *I'll be in The Giant's Club at Cerne tonight and again tomorrow night*, it said, without greeting or signature. When he went down again, he walked through the rear part of the house and left by the boot-room door, but not before taking a jacket and a pair of motorcyclist's goggles from the pegs there. The jacket was Spanish leather lined with sheepswool, with a generous collar. Charles had paid too much money for it in London and was as proud of it, almost, as he was of his motorbike.

Jack Yeoman took the Zenith from its shed, wheeled it down the drive keeping to the verge and watching over his shoulder, and when he got to the spinney, he kick-started the machine and drove away.

All the road long by Ibberton and Woolland, the shells were bursting behind the hedges and the rattle of gunfire was chasing him down the lanes and in his nostrils once more was the smell of cordite and filth.

6

But he left it behind as he went up Bulbarrow Hill, where along the top blew the Bulbarrow wind, as if the hill had its own familiar wind that blew only here. He stopped, wanting to sit for a while in this familiar wind and look out over the Vale. He left the bike on the turf and stepped downhill to get away from the road, and here there were overgrown tussocks of grass that he sat against comfortably, looking out at the land between his bent knees.

This was really the heart of Dorset, this high ridge of Bulbarrow, with Rawlsbury Camp to the west and the valley of Woolland laid out perfectly below. No one else makes hedges quite like this, he thought, as he looked down across the patchwork of fields, some still green, others stubble white, and the dark lines of hedge like the intricate seams of a great garment worn by the land. From here he could see as far as West Hill at Sherborne and beyond that, too, towards Glastonbury Tor. And these places ought to have changed as he himself had changed, but it seemed that they had not. From here, you couldn't make out a road or a car or a telegraph pole or a railway track. There were only the fields and woods and hedges and a cottage here and there, and there was no way of saying for sure what century this was, any more than he could say when the wind would cease blowing against his face. The tussocks made good pillows, and the wind sang a delicate song through the grasses and the gorse, and among these easy pillows and this fine music, the soldier slept.

He dreamed of a great head lying on the land and at first he wouldn't look at it supposing it to be a head among millions, severed and disfigured. Then he saw that its beard was forest and its wrinkles were tracks, and earthen mounds made cheeks and chin. Its teeth were of stone and its eyes were lakes and its nostrils were caves. It was crowned with a band of fire. As he watched, the head rose from the land, hauling upward a dark body of scorched grass and withered trees, and from the shadowed lands of its torso an arm lifted aloft a massive black club. From all around and below it, from the houses and churches and fields, a cry went up which had more of adulation than fear.

It was the cold that woke him much later, and he set off southwards towards Cerne. The chill air clutched at his face. Out of the dark came the villages, first a stray cottage, then rows of uneven dwellings huddled together. A yellow glow came from behind the curtains, from worlds inaccessible. He stopped by a curtainless window where an old woman was bent over a table, reading by candlelight. He was inexplicably touched by the sight. Then she glanced up in surprise, and a fearful look crossed her face. He wanted to pull off his goggles and explain, but no explanation was possible so he drove on.

Behind the houses grew the black hillsides and the trees met over the road, blotting out the stars. He took the track leading up to the ridge above Cerne. It grew colder. The hills were no more than a few hundred feet of limestone rising from the clammy loams, yet there was the true feel of the uplands. A half-moon shone in a velvet sky and the land glinted back. Tall clumps of beech stood along the top of the ridge, and burly hawthorns squatted around the track, bent backwards by relentless winds out of the west. The track was narrow and the land fell steeply away on either side. It was as if he rode along the spine of some huge beast that might rear up and throw him off.

The way to Cerne dropped steeply downwards between high hedges that hid the moon and the fields both, leaving a scarf of midnight blue above his head, shot with stars. The track was thrown up in deep ruts and the wheels of the bike jarred in the furrows of clay. *There's a road to heaven and a road to hell, but damn the road by Kiddle's Bottom*, the locals said. His father Louis must have told him that, for he liked such country speech, and Jack smiled to remember it as he drove into the old town of Cerne, where the houses of Abbey Street rolled the sound of the motor to and fro between them. He parked the bike by the wall of *The Giant's Club* and went inside.

There were three men in the taproom, and each one of them looked up at the newcomer, but no one spoke a greeting, and the greeting that Jack would himself have given waited an instant too long and then was too late to be said. They were wary of him because he was a stranger, and he was still wary of himself.

He asked for a beer and caught sight of himself in the mirror behind the bar. What he saw astounded him. His eyes had retreated under his brow, and there was something deep inside them like a winter sea or the ashes of a fire. His reflection was joined in the mirror by the back of the landlord's head and for a moment this too riveted his attention, the ripples of flesh above the collar, the greying wisps of hair. There was something sad in it, as if what was mirrored behind him was the man's fate, of which he would be forever unaware.

The landlord set down the beer.

'Travelling far?' he said.

'Not far,' he answered, and took his drink over to a seat by the open fire. He thought he could feel eyes on him, but he was wrong about this, for they were polite as well as wary, these Cerne folk, and if he had no business with them, then their business was to have none with him. He sat and tasted the first English ale he had drunk for six months in front of the first log fire he had seen since the night when he had put his uniform on, and Maggie Fox had called him the handsomest soldier in Dorset. He drank the beer fast and it seemed to him very strong. He watched the flames of the fire perform their repertoire of tricks, leaping and twisting on invisible shafts, shooting in thin tongues into the charred hollows, setting chains of sparks to run up the flanks of logs or flicking them into the air where they gleamed before disappearing darkly up the chimney. He picked up the blackiron poker that lay by the fire and thrust it at the incandescent logs, watching as they split open in blooms of red cinders.

The door opened and in came Bill Bate, the second of the six. He was a big man, not tall, but broad of back and forearm, and he moved like one needing an effort to contain his strength within the limits of his frame. The drinkers at the bar spoke their greetings, and Bill Bate looked them over with a quick glance, and his glance took in Jack too. One man had moved from the stool at the end of the bar and Bate took it. The landlord lifted a pewter tankard from its hook and filled it with a pint of darkish bitter with no head and set it on the bar in front of Bill Bate, who said: 'Pour one for the lad with the poker, to see if we can get a story from him.'

The drink was poured and delivered, and the soldier raised his glass to the man at the bar, who nodded at him and watched him drink. What the man saw was a boy with a good-looking face and dark skin, with large, brown eyes under a broad forehead and jet black hair. The brow and the chin and the eyes were those of a man in his mid-twenties, and Bate was not sure exactly what it was about him that was younger than that. Something about his body, a juvenile unease.

'That don't look like an army haircut you're wearing,' Bate said, 'and that ain't no ordinary machine you've got waiting in the yard, so it ain't no ordinary tale you've got to tell, I'm betting.'

'Pretty ordinary for these times, if I was to tell it,' said Jack.

'I'm right though, aren't I? No army would put up with a haircut like that.'

'Only an army in which the barbers who haven't lost their scissors have lost their heads.'

This remark silenced even Bill Bate. Jack took a swallow of beer, watching them at the bar.

'When the barbers lose their heads,' he said, 'it isn't the end of the world. But when the politicians and the generals lose their heads, the world's end may be getting close, and you might neglect to get your hair cut according to the prevailing customs.'

'The prevailing custom around this neck of the woods,' said Bill Bate, 'is to stick up for your country right or wrong, and to my way of thinking it's not the heads of the politicians that need seeing to but the stomach of those doing the fighting.'

'Go out there and fight then.'

'I was planning on doing just that, sonny, but they took against this.' The man held up his right hand with the fingers standing, and there were only three and the thumb, with a gap where the index finger should have been. 'That's the one that would have pulled the trigger, see, but I would have been happy to pull the trigger with this one ... ' – he folded his other fingers and left only the middle one upright, and he left it like that as he went on, with his hand next to his big face and the middle finger raised – ' ... or I would have put the gun to my other shoulder and fired it cack-handed. Or I would've got close enough to do the job with the bayonet.'

Jack looked back at the fire, and watched a new flame spurt up a patch of dried algae grown on the bark of an oak log.

'If you knew what it's like, you wouldn't talk the way you do,' he said. 'The job of the bayonet is butchery done on creatures that cannot be eaten and who do not run away.'

'Some do,' said Bate quick and sharp as a knife.

The two of them exchanged a look then which said all that needed to be said between them, because the soldier would not deny what he had done. Bate, for all his bluster, had keen eyes in a keen head, and only learned then what his instinct had told him from the start. He fell silent, turning back to the ale on the bar in front of him, grasping the mug with the hand that lacked a finger and taking it to his lips with satisfaction, knowing the sweetness of bitter. Jack considered how very short a time it had taken him to reveal what he should not have revealed, and to this man of all men. It was as if there was written on his face: *This man threw away his rifle and left.* But really he didn't care who knew it, because it was the truth. He took the dice from his pocket and tossed them on the table in front of him.

In a corner of the room, a grandfather clock ticked the long seconds. No one spoke, and the clock had the field to itself, tirelessly tick-tocking, as if there was nothing to the unrepeatable seconds but the marking of them. The taproom of *The Giant's Club* was built in the days when the market at Cerne was the busiest between Dorchester and Sherborne. Two or three score farmers had passed through the doors of the inn on a market day, as well as ploughmen and hedgers and foresters and shepherds, and the handful of butchers who bought most of the livestock. All the lambs and calves from the valley of the Piddle and the surrounding hills had passed through the pens at Cerne. But the railways ran fresh arteries through the body of the land and so the abbey town of Cerne missed out on the passengers and the freight, the flat wagons of lumber and steel, the coal stores and timber yards, the station hotels and the race meets. Cerne stayed where it was with both feet in the middle ages and its head in the air between Giant Hill and Black Hill, and its quiet, polite streets with the weeds showing among the cobbles. Seventeen hundred and ninety-four said the date on the longcase clock in the corner of the taproom, and when the clock sounded its first tick, Cerne might have been on its way to be as busy as Dorchester or as rich as Sherborne, but it was not to be.

The latch of the outside door rasped and lifted. All eyes went to the heavy door as it opened and there entered a young woman alone, an unusual event in *The Giant's Club* at any time and almost unprecedented on a winter night. She stood at the door and spoke a good-evening to the men at the bar in a voice which carried a kind of perfect clarity, like a bell. She wore riding britches and riding boots and a tweed hacking jacket as if she'd come on horseback, but it was on a bicycle she'd ridden several miles through the dark. Her hair was long and black, tied in a ponytail, her cheeks rosy from the ride. It was not her appearance, however, that struck the men at the bar so much as her stillness and composure before a company of strangers.

This was Maggie Fox, the third of the six, who had found Jack's note on her pillow and had come as she was bid. She saw him getting to his feet by the fireplace and went to him. He was thinner, she saw, and tauter and sadder. All of which she expected, but you don't know how such things will look until you have seen them. His clothes hung loose at the waist and his head seemed too big for his body, like a young rook. He would not embrace her in front of people, she knew, so she touched him on the arm and sat down and asked him to get her a lemonade. He called out for it in his bass voice and until the landlord brought it they sat in an uneasy silence and she wondered at the awkwardness there was between them, who were brother and sister practically.

She thought that the uneasiness was shared by the men at the bar, and she was correct in this, because the ripples of Bill Bate's *"Some do!"* (sharp and quick as a knife) had barely subsided, and no small talk had intervened. On the table, she saw two dice, one red and one white, and these had something to do with it, she felt obscurely.

'You're looking fine, Maggie Fox,' Jack said.

'And you too, Jack Yeoman. Though you've not been eating enough it seems and a drop of sunshine wouldn't do you any harm.' She wondered whether these weren't frivolous words for a man back from the war and, looking at him to find out, she saw in his eyes the shadow that he had seen in the mirror, the ash-like remnant of something burnt.

On the black beam above the bar were horse brasses and bright snaffles and crownbands and cockades, from the days when the London mailcoach used to call, leaving Exeter the day before and getting in to Cerne in the small hours sounding its horn to call the stableboy from his bed, and there was hot tea for the driver at that very bar, and for the passengers too if they woke, and the stableboy would take out the team of six horses that had pulled the mail over the hills and put in the new team that would take it as far as Salisbury. Three times a week for two hundred years, the yard was alive with the jostle of the big animals and the rattle of the harness and ringing of the ironshod hooves on the cobbles. Now there was neither stableboy nor groom nor any jostling horse in yard or stall. Just the three drinkers at the bar and the landlord behind it.

The men turned from the scene at the fireplace and struck up a conversation. Each day the matter of the war was the talk in the tap-room of *The Giant's Club*, and even without maps or co-ordinates the men knew what was Loos and the Somme, and why the French had fought such a bloody battle to hold Verdun. They were familiar with a three-inch mortar and a field howitzer, perhaps picturing them wrongly in terms of barrel and breech, but still appreciating their part in the campaigns and, since they knew the work of ploughing on heavy fields, well able to imagine the task of using horses to haul these iron monsters through the mud.

Bate was at the centre of their military deliberations. The bailiff on the estate brought in copies of the *War News* that the squire had finished with and Bate would pore over the pictures and their captions, becoming familiar with the names of regiments and battles, and repeating them aloud to his drinking partners, as if he believed that his steady, vociferous support for the armies of the Empire would make a difference. And who can be sure that it did not?

On this night, the talk at the bar settled on the question of what sort of man made a good officer, with Bert Moon opining that officers did not command the respect of their men unless they were born to it, and Frederick Rose, landlord and butcher, holding that it had nothing to do with breeding.

'To my way of thinking, it's what's wrong with the army. Your gentry get the pips on their shoulders and your working man don't earn more than a sergeant's stripes. Some of them young captains in there,' he said, gesturing at the pile of *War News* on the bar, 'look like they couldn't say boo to a goose in a lane, and there's no jaw on 'em to speak of. The lines of a man's face do show the working of his will, and an officer should 'ave a strong jaw and strong shoulders before he can tell another man what to do. I'd rather take orders in the field from you, Bill Bate, than I would from some dainty gent, although I might settle on 'im to draw up a deed or explain why the planets don't stay in the same place. Horses for courses, Bill, and the battlefield's not the place for dressing up or book-learning.'

'There's an easy way of speaking that gentry do,' said Bate, 'along with a cold way of looking with the eye, and these ways seem like power even when they ain't. I don't know how it's done and I wouldn't want to learn, but maybe the army reckons you can't do an officer's job without 'em.'

The bottom half of William Hart's right ear was missing, shot off by a sniper's bullet in the Cape. 'I've seen young gents who you'd say looking at 'em wouldn't know how to shave their beards, and sometimes who had no beards to shave,' he said, 'but I've seen these boys give orders to men of twice their brawn and bull without the blink of an eyelid and I saw one of them at the heart of the battle stand and fight in a kind of pit with only enemies round him, and he slashed one head almost right off and shot another one through the throat and came out of the pit and fought on. I reckon I was the only one to see that because I never heard tell of it after, although it was the bravest piece of fighting that I ever saw. It means, see, that he never told of it, nor thought much of it perhaps. And that's gentry for you, or part of it. Bain't nought to do with birth. 'Tis about ownership, and the way I know this is because the Boers were fighting for themselves and for their land and it didn't make no difference among the Boers whether they was corporal or colonel. They all fought the same way because it was their pride to do it.'

'You mean to say that a man's only got pride if he's got land or a title?' boomed Bate, thumping the bar with his fist.

'I mean you need a stake to play the game to the end, and the higher the stake the harder you'll play,' Hart said. 'The gentry 'ave got the bigger stakes. That's about the size of it, I reckon.'

'War's not a game,' said Bate to have the last word. But there was something in what Hart said that made him uneasy, an issue he hadn't grappled with. He briskly downed the half-pint that remained in his mug, and the speed of the downing fired him up. He turned towards the soldier, getting ready to re-open his attack in that quarter, when Jack's voice was suddenly raised, saying '*I will not go back.*'

They heard it at the bar and each of them at once caught the force of this declaration. The reaction of Bert Moon was to comment on the weather, which he said was getting ready for a good blow in a day or two, because the rooks had taken to roosting in the lower field, a thing he hadn't seen since the storm that took off the old king half-a-dozen years before. The landlord wanted to know whether a gale in middle

17

Dorset had blown away King Edward VII at his palace in London, and Moon said that wasn't what he meant but that kings don't die without the weather giving some sign of it.

'Twaddle,' said the landlord.

'Take my word for it,' Moon asserted. 'Wild weather be a portent.'

Bill Bate was looking at the soldier with an unblinking stare that said as clearly as words that no man might utter such a sentence in his hearing without explaining himself.

'I will not go back,' Jack said again, meeting his stare.

'Get up and say that,' said Bill Bate, sliding off his stool and standing squarely by the bar.

Jack stood up and said it for a third time. Sitting beside him, Maggie watched one of his hands gripping the other and both of them twisting together behind his back. She did not believe that it was fear, so it was the experience of war that had screwed something tight inside him. His easy way with life was gone, and she wondered whether it was forever.

'I'm glad to see that you're a big lad,' said Bate. It had surprised him to discover that Jack was a head taller than himself. 'Because if I have to put you right about your duty, I shan't be so feared of doing you a hurt as I might if you were a tiddler.'

'These people,' Jack said to Maggie, 'seem to feel that a man should lay down his life without protest. This man in particular,' indicating Bate, 'thinks that it is a man's duty to go uncomplaining to his death, whether or not there is good reason for it. Am I right, sir?'

'Jack, hush, there is no need for this,' Maggie said, but he ignored her.

'Take July the first,' he said. 'I haven't heard the figures because I've been away, and even if I had heard them they'd be lies, of the kind that generals must always tell for the good of us all, so I don't know whether it was tens of thousands that died or just thousands, so let's say thousands. Most of these died in holes or puddles and most of them didn't complain much, because what complaint can a man make against a hundred pounds of high explosive dropping from the sky or the path of a bullet he never saw? What do you think, sir?'

The big man at the bar shifted his position but made no answer.

'Thousands of Englishmen and Scotsmen and Welshmen – and Germans – all died uncomplaining in one day, so why should I be the one to complain, who am still alive? That's the real question, isn't it, why shouldn't I get on back there and die with the rest? But you see, the dead can't complain so the living have to do it for them, or they'll be killed in their turn leaving no one.'

'Steady lad,' said the landlord. 'It were a rum deal right enough, but don't dwell on it. You're getting rather confused, p'raps.'

There were nods of agreement at the bar. He was confused.

'Confusion! The very name of the game! We didn't know north from south or right from left. Once I saw a man unable to decide which boot went on which foot. I put them on for him and laced them up but he still wasn't sure, looking at them as if he were standing back to front.'

'We could leave now, Jack, if you want,' Maggie said.

'Back to front, you see,' he went on. 'That's how I must have been standing when I walked away.'

19

'Maybe he should be getting along, Miss,' said the landlord. 'Seems like he's a bit upset.'

'Upset and confused. Yes. How understanding of you. More understanding than the army will be, that's for sure. You see they have very little idea of how upset and confused a man can get in those rat holes, because they've worked out all the specifications, all very careful – how wide to dig and how deep, quantity of duckboards and sandbags, field telephones, bunk holes and funk holes. Well-planned and snug, they think, so if a man has had enough and walks off, it's inexplicable. But it does happen, in exceptional cases, so there needs to be something in the regulations, an official explanation. Confused and upset doesn't have the right military ring to it, so shellshock is what they come up with; they're big and noisy those artillery shells and sometimes it seems as if the popping and the banging and the thundering will never ever stop, which is a thought that even staff officers grasp. But shellshock is still too dramatic and unscientific and besides it fails to explain why this person should get it and that person should not. That's where LMF comes in. LMF has everything the army requires: obviously it's scientific – because otherwise it would consist of words, like ordinary speech. Instead of that it has only three letters, not to be confused with LMG, which is light machine gun, or LGM, which is light grenade mortar, or LMGH, which means let-me-go-home. No, LMF means Lack of Moral Fibre, an unexceptional way of describing an exceptional condition, a decent way of describing the indecent.'

Maggie had her hand on his sleeve and when he stopped speaking, she squeezed his arm with her fingers, but he shook her off.

'Once these three insidious little letters are written down against a person's name, the appropriate disciplinary action can be taken without compunction, naturally, and that person soon becomes an LMF casualty, by means that I do not need to go into. I don't believe that they've got round to abbreviating this to LMFC as yet, to make it even neater and more decent, but that will come I expect, as the years pass and the cases multiply and the army grows more adept at making the personal impersonal. Lance-Corporal Jack Yeoman LMFC. It will look all right on my tombstone, I feel. What do you think, Maggie?'

'What I think,' said Bill Bate loudly, 'is that you should shut your gob.'

'We had a sergeant like you, sir, until he got his foot blown off, and that was always his way of putting a stop to upsetting or confusing kind of talk. "Shut yer gobs!" he would say, and we did, him being a bullying and desperate sort of person, with three stripes on his sleeve. He was just the right type for keeping order in the ranks, keeping the lid on as it were, because if the lid comes off ... '

'If the lid comes off, we'll be supping German soup,' said Bill Bate.

'Nicely put, sir, and not at all confusing. Just what my brother would say. You should meet the captain. You'd get on famously, I'm sure.'

'I think,' said Maggie Fox, 'that we should be going home now.'

She got to her feet and looked at Jack, pleading, but he wouldn't meet her eye. Instead he grabbed up the dice from where they lay in front of him and cast them hopping and skittering over the table top. He swept them up again so swiftly that she had no chance to see what they showed.

'You're right. We should go,' he said, going to the bar. 'What's the score, landlord? I'd best pay for both of the beers. Wouldn't be right for someone like me to take a drink from someone like him.'

Two beers and a lemonade made fivepence, the landlord told him.

'I offered the drink and I'll pay for it,' said Bill Bate. He pulled a battered purse from his pocket and slapped two pennies down on the bar. 'The story wasn't worth tuppence, 'tis true, nor even a ha'penny, nor aught at all, but it's him that'll pay for it in the end, I'll be bound.'

'Then I thank you for the drink and wish you good riddance,' said Jack, handing over his three pennies.

Bill Bate moved between Jack and the door.

'Good riddance it had better be,' he said. 'I'll not be expecting to see you in these parts come tomorrow, or ever after that. It's lucky you're a pretty gabber, with your long words and tricks, because you'll be needing them for the court-martial. My name's Bate. They all know me in this neck of the woods, from the squire to the squirrels. Not that the squirrels are much interested in the likes of you, but I daresay the squire will want to know what kind of trash the wind have blown in, and I'll see to it that he does. I've got the name, Jack Yeoman, and your brother's rank, and if I could nail down the place you come from it might help, but t'wont make much difference in the long run.'

'I don't see that it's any of your business,' said Maggie Fox, astonishing all of them.

Bill Bate turned his eyes on her and something angry started to his lips but he checked it when he saw her, because there was that composure to her, and the terrific clarity of her voice, and he was ashamed to threaten her as he would threaten a dog with a stick.

'Maybe you don't, young lady,' he said, 'but this here is between men and it'd be better if it stayed that way.'

'It's between him and his brother and me,' Maggie Fox said.

'Then if I were you, I'd make sure that he keeps going on that motor of his when he gets it started up, because he'll need to put a few miles between himself and Bill Bate before he turns in.'

Bate made just enough room for the two of them to get to the door, and as Maggie Fox squeezed past him, she saw his face close up, thrust forward, bullish. It was a face round and blunt, more hammer than chisel, but there was an odd beauty in the brow and the eyes, as of one who pondered and felt. It surprised her to see that Bill Bate was a good-looking man.

Chapter Two

Witchwing

That these little things should carry such luck, and such charm, and such a spell, and such power in 'em, passes all I ever heard of or zeed.   (Thomas   Hardy)

THE moon had gone behind clouds and the yard was very dark. The inn sign swung and creaked in the wind. Jack told her to leave her bicycle and climb up behind him on the Zenith.

'Where are we going?' she asked.

'To see my father,' he said. 'Put your arms round me, Maggie, and cuddle up close. It'll be cold.'

To see his father, he said, but his father was dead and he didn't know it. She should have told him that instant in the dark, windblown yard, but she could not. She got up behind him and they started off. For a blessed time, the rest of the world was lost in the comfortable rumble of the motor as she clung to Jack Yeoman, feeling small and safe and full of a love that might burst out if she didn't hang on tight. By the side of the road, the silhouettes of houses gave way to the silhouettes of trees. The dark mass of Giant Hill grew and subsided and other hills loomed up and sloped off into the dark.

Maggie Fox loved Jack Yeoman, and not like a sister loves. They'd been her family for fourteen of her twenty years – Louis, Charles and Jack – but Jack she loved in a special way, which she had always kept to herself. Now Louis was dead and when they got to the cottage she would have to tell him.

24

She peered over his shoulder and watched the headlamp cast its funnelled gleam on the black surface of the road, like a blind man's stick. The blind postman at Margaret Marsh knew the footpaths like the badgers knew them, Louis had said. The thought of the lightless world inhabited by the blind postman made the faint gleam seem brighter as the bike sped along the road. Around them, the dark grew large.

'The night is so steep to climb,' she had once said to Louis (so he had told her) when she had been unable to sleep, a small child still unfamiliar with her new home, adrift in the big house and uneasy under the high ceilings. 'Our orphan Maggie', the kitchen maid called her, but she wasn't that, because her father had gone away, not died but just gone away. 'Poor old Will Fox,' Louis would say of her father, 'swept off by a wave bigger than his courage.' Later when she wanted to hear her own story, he had said that her father had left her because it was the only way he saw ahead of him. 'William Fox was an insubstantial fellow,' he told her, 'but there are many worse than he, and he did not leave before he knew you would be cared for, perhaps better than he could do it himself. You can be sure, Maggie, that he left with a bitter heart and some great wound inside of him that won't ever heal.'

On a steep climb between high banks, the motor coughed, spat and stopped. She got off while Jack kicked at the starter. The engine fired then failed. They found a battery torch in the saddlebag and Maggie held it while Jack prodded in the fuel tank with a twig, which came out dry.

'We'll leave it and walk,' he said.

How calm he was. She thought they should get the bike off the road and hide it, but he wasn't bothered. 'It'll come to no harm right where it is,' he said.

They started walking. He warned her it might be two hours to Louis's place.

'I can walk as far as you, and you know it,' she said.

The trees were high on either side and there was no moon in the sombre channel of sky. They breasted the hill and descended again between the black walls of trees.

'Jack the gabber, Jack the gadder,' she said, touching his shoulder with her fingers.

He put his arm around her and squeezed her to him. In a moment of happiness, as if fallen on them like a sudden dew, they walked on through the boundless dark. As long as this night lasted, they were together, she thought, and she wished that it might not be two hours but twenty, or that this walk might by some miracle prove to be their whole life, long or short, if only they might walk it side by side.

Around them the trees thinned and a larger sky came back and soon they made out the outlines of buildings before them. He was hungry he said, so she told him she had bread and cheese and apples. They came among the buildings, one of which was a great barn with a low-slung roof and tall double doors ajar. They were drawn in for the warmth and inside the air was sweet with the summer hay stacked to the rafters. They crouched on a bank of hay and Jack took off his brother's jacket, so warm it was among the bales. She broke the bread and the cheese and passed most of it to him, and they ate all the food with one apple each, then drank the lemonade from the flask.

Now she must tell him about Louis.

'Jack … ' she began.

From the far end of the barn, there came the neighing of a horse, followed by snorting and stamping.

'We can take two of the horses and ride to Louis's place,' he said.

'We surely *cannot*,' she said.

'We've a long way to go, and there's a fog coming up the valleys.'

'I saw no fog.'

'You can smell it gathering down there on the brooks and the ponds. It'll be thick on the bottom road by Buckland. Horses don't bother about fog. They just keep on going.'

'We can't take someone else's horses, Jack.'

'Borrow. We borrow them for an hour and let them find their own way back. They'll be waiting here by the barn in the morning. At the front, there are horses pulling carts full of bodies and when the big shells come in, the horses scream in terror and get flung around the landscape in bits. What we're going to do is to borrow a couple of well-fed animals, treating them with every politeness and letting them stroll back to their owner afterwards.'

'This is the manor. They'll be the squire's horses.'

'Better take a horse from the squire who has plenty than from the carter who has one,' he said.

'Better not take any at all,' she answered.

'We'll ask the dice,' he said. She heard him reaching into his pocket.

'I don't like these dice of yours,' she said.

'The dice are a rational response to an irrational world,' he said.

'Maybe they're more of an addiction.'

27

It was always a free choice to throw the dice, he insisted.

'It looks to me like the opposite of choice,' she said. 'If you want to take the horses, then do it, even knowing it's wrong. But don't pass the responsibility on to a pair of wooden *fribbles*.'

'It was Louis who gave me them when I saw him before going to France,' he said. 'A talisman, he called them. I thought he was talking of luck, but he said that the currency of the dice was fate, not chance. It amounted to the same thing, I said, but he said, "Not at all it doesn't!" People were mistaken, he told me, in assuming that dice are the expression of random chance, and he pointed out that they knew deep down that it was not so. Everybody who casts a die feels the power of that little cube as it rolls over the table, he said, and when it shows what they want, they think "I knew it, somehow I knew it" and reckon they deserved it, for there is a connection between fate and deserving but between chance and deserving there is none. What about people who don't get the throw they want, I asked, but he said it was the same. Not my lucky day, they say out loud, but inside they feel that the dice has delivered a verdict on them. He talked about people who made a living out of gambling, the ones who can seemingly bend the die to their will or draw the card they want. There aren't many of those, I said, but he said they didn't need to be many to prove the point. If some men could overcome the laws of so-called chance, it meant that those laws were themselves not random. The opposition of chance and fate. "The dice will remind you of this," my father told me.'

There was the faint click of a switch and the beam of the torch made a miniature arena of light on the ground. Into this arena entered Jack's hand, clearing a space among the haystalks. All around it was black, and the small pool of light was very bright, a stage lit up in a theatre of dark. The two dice tumbled suddenly onto this lit stage, like acrobats sent on to start the play. They seemed to twine around each other as they fell through the air, then spun off in different directions when they hit the ground, leaping once and lying still. A pair of blockheaded clowns feigning life and death.

For a moment, he let them lie in the light. The pale upturned face of the white die presented a single black dot and the red die had the partially obliterated outline of the skull. The beam of the torch was switched off and she heard his hand gather the dice from the ground.

'Your father's dead,' she said.

She couldn't have explained why she said this now, why she had to be so abrupt, cruel almost. Perhaps she was irritated with him for fiddling with his infernal dice. But also she knew it was hopeless for her to draw the sting from what she had to say.

He made her repeat what she had said and something cold and flat came into his voice. He asked her when and how, which day, who was there. When he heard that it happened at night, he wanted to know if the light was on and when she said she didn't know, he insisted on this point as if it had some special significance that she could not fathom.

'Who found him?'

'Grammer Score.'

'I'll ask Grammer then. Tomorrow I'll find Grammer and ask her.'

'The doctor said he died in his sleep.'

'Then the doctor was wrong. Louis wasn't a man to be taken by Death in his sleep.'

'It was a stroke, the doctor said.'

'Yes. A stroke, a blow, an onslaught. That must have been so. And he fought against it. There was no one there even to hold his hand, so he had to fight his final battle on his own. In the dark, you say?'

'I don't know, Jack. I told you that I don't know.'

'Grammer will know. I'm glad that it was Grammer who found him. She understands such things.'

'What things?'

'Death. Grammer knows about the coming of Death.'

Obscurely, she felt that this was true. If anyone knew, it was Grammer Score.

'Sometimes I've thought that Grammer looks a little like Death,' he said. 'Death's sister perhaps.'

'Jack, that's a shocking thing to say!'

'Life is the brother of Death, or its wife, or husband. She is a very old woman who has touched Death. You can see that in her eyes. I'm glad it was her. She will tell me. Why don't I cry, Maggie? Why won't my eyes fill with the tears that I feel inside me?'

'Maybe there will come a time,' she said.

'We'll take the horses,' he said.

It was not right, she knew. It was all wrong. But she lacked the will to oppose him now.

'Jack, will they shoot you if they catch you?' she asked him instead.

'Dawn is the favoured time,' he said. 'A blindfold, a last wish. A final throw of the dice to choose one of thirty-six options for life after death. There's a wall at the camp in Aldershot, they say, pitted with bullets at head height. Good name for it, Aldershot. Given its name by the army in Victorian times. Along with Bagshot, Oxshott and Shotem

30

Down.'

'You can hide out at the cottage,' she said. 'Nobody need see us go in or out. Why didn't you tell me to meet you there? Why did you make me come all the way over to Cerne?'

'The dice said so.'

'Do you ask them everything?'

'Not everything.'

'Jack, I will come with you wherever you go. I will do whatever you ask of me. If you want me to lie for you, I will lie for you. But put away the dice. I will not be ordered by the whims of painted cubes. I will not do it.'

'We must take the horses, or spend the night in the fog,' he said.

He turned on the torch and she followed him to the far end of the barn. There were two horses tied up in adjacent stalls with doors opening directly to the outside. He directed the beam of the torch on each of them in turn: a young black filly with a narrow head and a heavier bay mare with a white flash on its brow.

'The black one for you and the bay for me,' he said.

The horses lay back their ears and stamped. Jack climbed into the mare's stall, untied the halter rope and made a makeshift rein. Maggie did the same with the black filly, speaking softly to her. The filly pranced back, flung up her head and whinnied. A dog began barking, and it was joined by another further off.

Jack got the door of the stable open and Maggie led out the filly, who jittered and reared.

'Steady, girl. Steady now,' Maggie told her.

Around them from the shadows, the sound of barking rose in pitch and volume. Maggie waited until the filly quieted and vaulted on to her back. The horses started off as if whipped from behind, and it was they who chose the way.

Maggie stretched all the way forward until her head was almost against the horse's shoulder. Woodland loomed on her right, then it was directly ahead of them and at once they were among trees, with branches sweeping by close above. The track began bending uphill and the horse slowed to a walk and Maggie sat up and looked over her shoulder.

'Jack?' she called out. And from a little way behind her Jack answered.

The path led up the hill's flank, obliquely at first, then turning sharply upwards so that the movement of the horses grew laborious; the angle of their bodies steepened and their breath came quicker and louder. At the top, Maggie's horse stopped, and Jack's behind her, and they were on a ridge of hill between woods. Above them the moon came out and when Maggie looked up to the sky she saw a spangled realm of ragged cloud foiled with silver.

He saw the same clouds but to him they were bursts of smoke discharged by cannon, taken aloft by the wind and hanging like parachutes in an embattled sky. Only the noise was absent that should have been there, the boom and the thunder and the blast near or far, and it occurred to him that he had gone deaf. How would he hear the whistle of the shell as it careered earthwards towards him? How would he know when to flatten himself against the mud wall? His moment of panic spooked the horse and she started suddenly forward along the ridge. He was back in the battle he had never really left, and when he felt the horse moving underneath him, it made no sense to him that he was horseborne, unless this was how the souls of the dead were carried into the hinterlands of what lay beyond.

They lost the track and soon after they lost the moon. They came to woods that might have taken them back up to the highway but wouldn't. The masses of the trees and the narrow paths plunged down and pressed west, whereas it was eastward and upward they wanted. They wanted Buckland and Hammond and what they got was Urley Moor and Middlemarsh.

At night the marsh grew large, the mires were black as oil and the deep ditches lay serpentine under the withies and the bog willows. Out of this tricky old marsh, that night of 30 October 1916, came a fog that hardly moved from the water, breathing just a few puffs of vapour up into the woodlands that flanked the hills. Over the marsh itself it was viscous thick, gathering into itself the emanations of the bog. Not even the eye of a cat could tell where earth and mist met, and only horses could have picked their way between the brimful fens masquerading as meadows.

Along these paths, the horses ridden by Jack Yeoman and Maggie Fox went by instinct, as horses will.

Jack came down from the aerial bombardment on the hills to a noman's-land with the dead waving soundlessly from the sodden ground, a swamp of skeletons that tried to lift themselves up and out. He was riding to his own death or through it, guns all quiet now, helmet gone, badges buried and trenches empty, only now this silent sea of the waving dead. Maggie Fox gone too, ooohh long gone.

The horse Maggie rode, to whom she had given the name Sylph for its high spirits and light feet, this Sylph came abruptly to a dead halt, ears cocked. Out of the fog came the sound of a dog barking, then once more, from somewhere else it seemed, for there were no directions in this muffling shroud worn by the mire. Then a man's curt voice calling out to the dog.

'Advance one and be recognised,' Jack shouted from the shores of the Somme, or the Styx.

One advanced, with caged lamp dangling from his hand, shotgun over his shoulder and dog at his heel.

'Hush, French,' the man told his dog.

'We're looking for the highway,' said Maggie Fox.

It seemed that the man would make no answer.

'Follow me then,' he said at last. 'And follow me close.'

'Your dog is making my horse nervous,' said Maggie.

'More likely it is you that is doing so,' he retorted. 'There's reason enough. Last week a man rode his horse into the bog and spent the night trying to get out. He was here in the morning covered in black slime like an eel in a ditch.'

'Then show us the way, if you please,' said Maggie.

'That's what I said,' the man said, leading off.

Man, dog and lamp dinked eerily among twisted willows. Maggie could hardly see ahead, only a paler patch where the lamp glimmered. The marsh stretched indefinitely around them and the track wound in its midst. Not once did their guide turn and call or acknowledge their presence, which Maggie Fox began to think was uncivil until she reckoned where they might have ended without him. Finally she saw another light ahead and scarcely had she seen it than it was upon them, hanging from a hook on a wall and above it the eaves of a house.

'We'll stop here,' said the man.

'There's no need for that, I hope,' said Maggie.

'What you hope is of little consequence,' he said. 'It's the fog that calls the tune tonight. It will be thicker still where you're going.'

Truly the fog was dense. He was standing only a few yards from her but still she could see no more of him than the glow from the lantern. He pushed open a double door behind him. The flame of the lamp leapt up brightly in the doorway and she caught her first glimpse of the man holding it. Gaunt, disdainful. Then he was gone inside the stable.

She turned to Jack, who was still at large between sword and skull. 'We should leave as soon as we can,' she whispered.

'Is this you with me here?' he said in a hollow, lost voice.

She looked at him quickly and chided him because he scared her. 'Jack don't you go dreaming now, it's not the place for it. *Is this me with you here* ... and who else would it be?'

Behind them, the dog called French growled softly.

They dismounted and led their horses into the stable. A piebald stallion in one of the stalls looked up to inspect them before returning to its hay. There were other stalls, all empty. A row of battered saddles and cobwebbed bridles told that the stables had been busy, once upon a time.

The man set his lamp on a barrel, broke open his shotgun and pocketed the cartridges. He snapped the gun shut and shouldered it.

'A bird don't tweet on Urley Moor without John French getting wind of it,' he said. He watched them as they saw to their horses. 'Throw them hay from the stack,' he said. 'And tie them close. The

35

stallion is no gentleman.'

When they were done, he led off through a door at the far end of the stable. The dog, a black and white border collie, watched them as they left before ducking back outside through a hinged flap of his own.

'You'll take the house as you find it,' the man said. 'It's not set up for guests.'

The stable connected with what had once been a dairy or pantry, with a long marble-topped table running down one side. The place smelled of damp and disuse. A bunch of long-dead flowers lay on the table, and empty bottles stood sentry on the sideboards. Afterwards came a scullery with a huge washbasin and drying racks against one wall, but nothing had been washed and nothing dried.

The heat from the next room hit them before they went in. A figure crouched over a fire that burned in one corner of the room. The man rose at once as they entered and with the slightest glance in their direction took himself off, picking up an axe from the top of a woodpile and disappearing noiselessly through another door.

'The slave doesn't care for strangers,' said the man who had brought them to this place.

The walls on either side were occupied by stacks of logs and sticks cut neatly to length. Three wooden stools and a couch losing its stuffing stood in a rough circle round the fireplace amid a litter of wood ash and flakes of bark.

The man put down his lamp and leaned his gun against the wall next to a second gun that stood there. He unbuttoned his long coat, which Maggie had taken for black in the gloom of the stable but now saw was a khaki trench coat, with brass buttons to the knee. He hung it from a hook behind the door. When he turned round, Maggie saw that he wore the reversed white collar and black surplice of a priest. A gold crucifix hung from his neck.

'I'd better know who I've got in my house,' he said.

Maggie glanced at Jack, who stood stiffly next to her, staring at the flames of the fire.

'This is Jack Yeoman and I am Maggie Fox,' the girl said. 'We lost our way between Cerne and ... Sherborne.'

'Long way in the dark without bridles,' the priest commented. 'Take off your coats and have a pew.' He gestured towards the couch.

Maggie sat on the edge of the couch and Jack perched woodenly on one of the stools. The fire that blazed in the corner was made of logs the size of a man's thigh which might have warmed a room of twice the size. By the barrel was a Welsh dresser with earthenware jars and bottles large and small stoppered with corks. A twist of garlic bulbs hung from a hook, and other pods and roots were twined or threaded in bundles and hung from the shelves.

The priest took a bottle from the dresser and filled two very small china cups with a liquid that glinted in the firelight. He passed one to Jack and offered the other to Maggie Fox.

'No, thank you,' said Maggie.

'Knock it back,' the priest told Jack. 'It's Urley gin, with sloes and cider apples and sweetroot and fennel seeds along with the malt.'

Jack drank it down and sat straighter on his stool, wrinkling his face and opening wide his eyes. The priest took back the empty cup and passed Jack the second one.

'You shall have tea,' he said to Maggie. He spoke without looking at her. He never looked at her, she noticed, or not for her to see it. But he was a priest. The collar and crucifix were a guarantee of ... something. Despite the guns and the trench coat and the gin.

He went to the fire and moved a tripod bearing a blackened kettle closer to the flames with the side of his foot. From the dresser he took a small teapot into which he put a pinch or two from the contents of three small jars. Later Maggie was to remember this gesture, which out of everything he did that evening stayed with her most particularly – this gesture of reaching up for the jars and putting a pinch or two from three of them into the little pot. In the light from the fire every-thing seemed made of copper. Copper teapot, copper jars, copper mug, the priest's scornful coppery face.

'What tea is that?' she asked abruptly. 'I prefer ordinary tea if it's convenient.'

'I don't use Indian tea,' he said.

'What do you use?' the girl asked.

'Herbs to sweeten the water and clear your noddle,' he said, as he filled the teapot from the kettle.

'What herbs?'

'Chamomile for sweetness, sage for clarity and thornapple for the wisdom of the wise.'

He stirred the pot.

'Are you not drinking, padre?' Jack said.

'Not tonight,' the priest said.

He squatted by the fire stirring the tea, poured a mugful and passed it to Maggie Fox. How thirsty she was suddenly. The tea was almost too hot to drink but very good. She perched on the decaying sofa and sipped at the drink without waiting for it to cool.

She drank her tea and there was a taste she couldn't place, bitterish but not unpleasant. She finished the cup and asked for another, which was bitterer. What was strange was how this bitter taste had started as the merest hint at the back and grown stronger as she drank. At first, it was the sage that was the driver of the brew, so to speak, and the chamomile that was the passenger, but this other taste came from behind and took over. It overpowered the driver and threw out the passenger, and was driver and carriage and horses at once. A sharp bitterness abruptly occupied the whole vehicle of her eyes and head and from this sharp bitterness she emerged hurtling wildly down a lane like a dark throat with the branches of the black trees twining overhead.

Maggie Fox rode swiftly away into a maddened land with voices knocking at the roof of her carriage and the elsewhere coming up through the floor like a flood. She wanted to run from it and felt the sensation of running in her legs but she could not move her limbs. She was aware of the two men in the room with her but a vast distance lay between her and them as if another world had intruded, the other world where the voices were speaking. She tried to make the room conform but it would not. The ceiling and roof seemed gone away. Then turned to turf as the room began to sink inside the earth.

She saw Jack and the man on stools in front of the fire. She saw Jack talking and the man observing him but Jack's voice could not come through. The lips moved but there was no sound. He was silently quacking like a dumb duck, caught in the intensity of the other man's lamps. Yes, *lamps*! The man's eyes glowed like lamps. There was a terrible restlessness in her legs. She thought she might step with huge strides from world to world, spring back and forth between the two. I am running without moving, she thought. I am a weed a-swhirl in the ocean.

It was the tea! The tea he had made so carefully with pinches of this and pinches of that and pinches of something else, to give her legs of sponge, sink the house and intrude this other world, while *he* insinuated by the fire … all the time eyeing poor Jack the gabber, like a rabbit in his lamps.

Jack's voice came through. 'Like rabbits in holes. We were like rabbits in holes, only worse because there was no jump left in us. *Over the top*! And over we went, no matter what. We went over with streaming colds and burning fevers that in any other life would have had us abed. We went over in rain and mud that keeps a farmer indoors. We went over with Death waiting out there in occupation of all and everything. He dressed in the uniforms, He was caught in the wire, He lived in the empty farmhouses, He dwelt in the mouth of the cannons and the bellies of the guns. He came out with the sun in the mornings and in the evenings He came out with the moon. With the rain He came and He kept close in the mists.'

'What versatility,' the priest commented.

'Over we went,' Jack said. 'Not out of courage or obedience but out of belief! Every one of us whether tall or short, hairy or smooth, bold or timid, caring or careless, every one of us once believed that our homes, our families, the flowers in the gardens and the babies in the cradles, depended on us taking up the rifle with its murderous blade and its slugs of lead. We were armed with the weapons of the Devil but we were fighting on the side of Christ. Not the Christ of the pulpit, padre, or of the sentimental paintings, but the Christ inside who keeps us turned towards the light. You know who I mean.'

'*I* do,' said Maggie Fox, but she couldn't tell whether she had really said it, and then she couldn't remember what it was she might have said. Was it 'I too'? Or was it one, two, sentinels of the entire series to infinity? One the single, the indivisible; two the pair, the double, the other. I am split in two, she thought.

The voices from elsewhere grew very loud, disputing at tremendous speed, so that whole conversations were achieved in an instant. I am awake in both places, she thought, as she returned to the sunken hull of the room.

'You know what I mean,' Jack Yeoman was saying.

'I do not,' said the priest, if priest he ever was. He was nothing like any priest she knew of. His collar was copper in the light of his infernal fire. There was a hardness about him, oh yes there was about him something very hard, the kind of creature you would hurt yourself on if you knocked against it.

'But *you* must know Christ,' Jack insisted.

'Christ the king or Christ the martyr?' the priest said, holding out his hand for Jack's cup.

'Still not drinking yourself, padre?' said Jack.

'I do not drink when I am studying,' said the other.

'And what might you be studying tonight?' Jack asked foolishly.

'I'm studying *you*,' said the priest without caution or remorse.

Jack laughed aloud and Maggie was angry because he carelessly drank with this dangerous person and failed to come awake even at the blunt warning, 'I'm studying *you*'. Yet it was not anger. No, no, no it was not anger but an undammable tide that flowed from her heart and from her very limbs, deeper than rivers, as deep as oceans and as large.

'Not another drink,' said Maggie Fox aloud, and this time they heard her from where she lay collapsed on the decomposing sofa, because they turned towards her. Jack's face bronzed in the light of the flames, framed in his rich black hair, and the other face furtively turned away as she looked. How and when did I lie down, she wondered, with my legs of live sponge? She could not distinguish what was the couch and what was herself, where one ended and the other began. Was she lying spongelike on the floor of this ocean? Was this a cushion beneath her or her own body gone soft?

'No more,' said Jack Yeoman.

'From what I keep for myself,' the priest said.

Jack glanced towards the couch before passing over his cup, and Maggie wished he hadn't done that. The priest took the cup from his hand, slunk towards the far door and vanished. She didn't see the door open or hear the click of the lock. No sound but the faint crepitation of the flames. No sign of the vanishing priest.

Jack sat mutely by the fire, his head and shoulders silhouetted against the glow of the flames. She read his thoughts in the slope of his shoulders. She told his mood in the curl of his hair. His shadow on the wall was more vivid to her than all the daylight flesh of another. Strides of sponge between worlds; the still-room of the priest creature sinking into the mire; the impenetrable blackthing pressed up against the window, Blackmister Night back after all these years; Jack's silhouette unmoving, made by fire.

The so-called priest slunk in with a small flask and squatted by the couch near Maggie's feet. He filled the cup and passed it to Jack and a little while later, his hand made its way into the pockets of the leather jacket thrown over the end of the couch, coming out with something clenched in it. There is not light enough to see it, Maggie Fox thought. I divine by his head that he caught something in the pocket. I saw the moment in the faintest turn of the head. I know what he has in the clutch of his paw.

'Just who is this?' The priest gestured towards Maggie Fox, helpless on the couch.

'This is Maggie,' said Jack Yeoman proudly.

They think I'm asleep, she thought. Are my eyes closed then? I see them clearly, the prince and the polecat. Am I seeing through my eye-lids?

'Why do you ride without saddles and bridles?' the priest asked, leaning forward.

I told you, she murmured. *I told you*. Actions have consequences. The creature is a consequence. His poisonous tea and insidious gin. His filching fingers. My legs feel like I will never lift them. And there's a space in space where the others were. The voices came from somewhere, didn't they.

There was a somewhere inside her, getting larger, blotting out the room and she felt she had gone upwards through where the roof had been. The fog had gone and the night was starry and she floated there.

Chapter Three

The Mandragorite … and His Slave

IN the back kitchen of Urley House, Jack Yeoman was fugged by the fire and giddy with the gin. Maggie Fox was asleep, which was good, and the man was fetching another little cup of that fiery liquor, which was very good, and nowhere had there been such a fine blaze. Like the very first fire, in the cavemouth on the mountainside. In anthropoid times. Anthropoid? I mean Cro-Magnitude times. The very first cavemouth fire in the Cro-Magnitude era of the antediluvian drift.

'One fire is all fires,' he said as the man passed him the tiny cup.

'Does that include the fires of hell?' the priest wanted to know.

'Perhaps the infernal fire is after all the first. No fires in paradise, are there, padre? Chilly up there among the clouds without a welcoming blaze. But you and me don't have to worry about that, do we. It'll be the other way for us. For me because I ran away and for you, because … because of your abandoned house and your rude animals and the skulls in the bog. I like your drink, but you do not have the look of paradise about you, padre. You are too … taut. Your face is too long. Forgive my bluntness. I have not much time. The niceties are running away from me, like children fleeing from a picnic in a storm.'

'You have as much time as any of us.'

'No. No. I do not. I am a deserter from the British army. I am a horse thief. I am motherless and now fatherless. If Louis were alive …

44

perhaps things might be ... but Louis is dead. ''Your father is dead,'' she said to me. And he was. That leaves brother Charles. But Captain Charles Yeoman MC is at his post, as always. Troops in the trenches. Animals in the farmyard. Makes no difference to him. Armies of cows and a platoon of old men leap to his commands and march in line over sodden fields. The tall barley salutes him in summer and in the autumn the potatoes are proud to give up their lives for him.'

'Not for him the flames of hell, then.'

'Charles? Charles has a highway straight to the pearly gates. A respectable road. Charles favours the respectful and the respectable. ''You are disrespectful, Jack,'' he says. And it is true! I am disrespectful of the highways. I prefer tracks that wind through woods and seek out hidden streams. I like the path to the pigsty where the mud never dries because of the leaking tap on the drinking trough. Charles fixed it once but it leaked again. ''It's *meant* to leak,'' I told him, which he told me was contemptible. Please be good enough to pour me one of your disrespectful and contemptible drinks.'

The priest whisked up the flask by his stool, poured a cup and passed it.

'The first of two,' he said. 'A double toast. One to celebrate the disrespect and one to mend the contempt.'

Jack Yeoman drank the first cup, screwed up his eyes and opened them very wide. 'It likes to do that,' he said, passing the cup for a refill. 'It likes to close you down and open you up. To a new world. To a newly recreated world. Same fire, same chips of wood on stone floor. But *wider* than before. It's the wider world, padre. Those chips of wood have acquired a larger identity. Chip off the old block. What do they mean by that? That I am like my father? Would that I were! I am surrounded by chips off old blocks. No chip of wood but has a parent. But I have none.'

'Your concern with yourself is feeble,' the priest remarked, returning the cup to him refilled.

Jack took the cup and emptied it in one swallow.

'Who are you to say so? You with your comfortable fire and your dry socks and the guns you will never use on anything more dangerous than a duck?'

'You consigned me to hell for the shape of my face. I shall also speak plainly. You are pathetic to feel sorry for yourself because your father died and because you envy your brother.'

'I do not envy my brother!'

'And you are proud because you are a deserter.'

'You are mad to say so.'

'According to the definitions of the highway, perhaps. But I assure you, you are envious of your brother the captain, and proud that you ran away from the trenches. Was it cowardice that made you do it?'

'It was not.'

'Then it was a rational response to an absurdity. It is not your desertion that makes you weak but the way you go about it. You pick up your girl, steal two horses and get lost in a fog. Tomorrow they'll come looking for you and when they find you they'll put you up against a wall and shoot you like a dog. No! Worse than a dog, which can die in a state of innocence and therefore with a kind of dignity. But there will be no innocence in the way you die. You are like a man who ties his own blindfold and walks towards the enemy with his hands out crying "Shoot me". I trust you will be proud of your martyrdom.'

'I have drunk enough,' Jack said.

The priest shrugged. 'Enough to discern the interesting situation of a wood chip. Not enough to discern your own, it seems.'

'Give me a glass of water.'

'There's water in the barrel in the scullery.' He gestured to the door they had come in by. 'Take the lamp and help yourself. If you can.'

The whereabouts of the lamp eluded him at first, then the finger-wheel for the wick turned the wrong way and snuffed out the flame. So he did without it, negotiating a tricky route across the room and struggling with the door, which caught him off balance by opening inwards. The scullery was grown larger and more forlorn. He encountered the barrel by the washbasin but the water had gone black in the dark and no mug came to hand. He located it at last, hanging from a hook above the barrel.

'So there you are, mug,' he said, dipping it into the dark water. He sniffed the water before drinking. Smells of nothing. Looks like nothing. Tastes like nothing. Thank the Lord for that. Adopts the colour of whatever is closest. He returned the cup to its place, despite the reluctance of the handle to accommodate the hook. 'Thank you, mug,' he said, when it was done. He cupped the palms of his hands, filled them with water and splashed his face, taking care that the drips fell to the floor and not back into the barrel. Mustn't dirty the man's drinking water. But my hands would have dirtied it already. When did I last wash them? He scooped out more water and rinsed his hands. One hand washes the other and both wash the face. Every small act of man so cleverly designed. Thank the Lord for that too. He put both hands to wash the face again, observing with satisfaction how each did its separate job oblivious of the other but in perfect harmony. Now the ears. Now the hair. Once more for the neck. Droplets journey downwards inside the shirt. Always heading downwards. Was this a clue? Find your way to the lowest place. Look like nothing, and return when you can to the underneath of everything. What had the priest said? Something true that had made him angry. Envious of his brother. Was it so? No, not that. Proud of deserting. A martyr. *That* was it. Proud to be martyred. Picked up Maggie, argued with the man at the bar, stole the horses. Everything to draw attention to myself. Am I seeking death then?

He returned smoothly to his place by the fire. The water that had restored him appeared also to have restored the world. A window stood open, bringing in whiffs of damp earth and wet moss. Jack Yeoman sat on his stool like a new man and when the priest passed him a drink a while later he put it down without drinking.

They sat in silence until the priest said: 'Deserters get caught because they wish to be.'

The lesson of the water was with him. He kept quiet.

'By tomorrow at noon you can be in a big city,' the priest said. 'Wear a uniform. Use another name. In cities money can be had. You will need to be ruthless, but ruthlessness is the only option in view of your inevitable death.'

'There is always more than one option, padre,' Jack said, pulling his jacket from the couch and searching its pockets.

'It is I who have the dice,' said the priest.

'You've damned well been through my pockets!'

'I have brought a deserter and horse thief into the house. I must be on my guard. Here, take them.' He took the dice from his own pocket and rolled them out on the seat of the empty stool, leaning forward to see what they read.

Jack swept up the dice, closing them in his fist. 'You had no right to take my private possessions from my jacket,' he said.

'Your private *obsessions*.'

'The dice are a game. Nothing more.'

'You neglected to bring a scarf for the cold or a purse for your journey, yet you did not neglect to bring your pair of curious dice.'

'I prefer that they are not handled by strangers.'

'Is that why you ignored my throw?'

'You threw Cross Three.'

'And its significance?'

Jack shrugged. 'It was your throw. Read it how you will.'

'Very well,' the priest said. 'Let us say that the three crosses is an image of the crucifixion.'

Jack looked at him sharply.

'Two criminals and Christ's representative,' the priest went on. 'The question is: Is the crucifixion foreseen by the dice symbolic or real?'

'You take the dice seriously.'

'The oracle should not be carelessly approached.'

'Even by the representative of Christ?'

'I did not indicate which of us that may be. My clerical garb is a mere convenience.'

'You are not a priest?'

49

'As much as you are a soldier.'

'You left the Church then.'

The priest poured himself a cup from the flask and drank it. He offered the flask to Jack, but when Jack shook his head the priest poured himself a second cup to follow the first.

'Which Church?' he said. 'Merlin is of more concern to me than Christ, and Puck than John the Baptist. I found more in Mistress Mab than in the Virgin Mary. Jesus of Nazareth was a desert Arab. A sandal wearer. But this is a land for *gumboots*. The gods of this land take shapes that shift like brooks slugging over marshes and darting down stony valleys. Their names change with their shapes. Robin Goodfellow is known in some parts as the Green Man and elsewhere as Hob or the Hobgoblin, who is also called Puck. The Green Man is a woodland king, but Puck is a maker of goblin devilry. So what is he? King Robin or Goblin Puck?'

'I supposed he was bred in the imagination of poets,' Jack said.

'Because your days until recently have been spent in comfortable sitting-rooms and the streets of polite towns,' the priest said. 'The forest people lived without carriages or schoolrooms, with the swine in the shed by the privy and the storms beating through the trees over their heads and the labour of every day taking them into the trackless forests among the deer and the wild boar. Their noses were full of the scents of bark and leaf-mould, and their eyes trained in the dim brindling light of the underwoods. Their gods wore horns or had heads like pigs and eyes like owls, and the acts of these gods were as real as trees that fell in storms or the bite of frost or the pinch of hunger. As they still are.'

'You are no Christian,' said Jack.

'I know the scream of the mandrake when pulled from the earth, like a babe newborn to the light of day. I am more Mandragorite than Christian.'

'You mystify me,' Jack said.

'Perhaps because you are not drinking,' he said. He went to the window and shut out the chill bittersweet air drifting in from the marsh.

'It takes speed to follow the paths where the gods lie concealed,' he said. 'In the correct measure, my Urley Gin is an accelerator. In excess, it is a drug.'

'Maybe a drug is what I need,' Jack said.

'You are drugged already. I see it in your eyes. You are drugged by a pointless Christian war. Drugged by the army and drugged by your dice. What you need is not more drugs but the will to give up the ones you have. The Cross Three need be no crucifixion for you. It is the three bridges you have to cross, the three decisions you must make.'

'Which are?'

'The first is to rid yourself of this insidious notion of home, somewhere you think you belong. Be gone from these parts, at once. The second decision is to give up the dice, and the third to abandon the vixen on the couch.'

'I will not abandon Maggie.'

'Then you will be shot. Alone in a city, Jack Yeoman can disappear. Here they will be looking for a young man and a girl on two stolen horses. How many such are to be found in the lanes and fields of this place? How long will it take them to find you? One day? Two? The company of the girl marks you out. Leave her asleep where she is. He travels fastest who travels alone. I will take you as far as the highway. You can be at the railway station in Sherborne before dawn. Turn the horse loose outside the town to find its own way home.'

'Why should I trust you?'

'What motive could I have beyond that of helping a man bent on suicide? When the girl awakes ... '

'Vixen, you said.'

'All women are foxes in cunning. When she awakes, there is food for her, a bed upstairs for the night. In the morning, she can ride home.'

He is right about Maggie, Jack thought. I should not have brought her to this. Is he right about me, too? A man bent on suicide.

'We are not unalike, Jack Yeoman. Like you I have no parents. Like you I deserted a meaningless existence. In you I see something of myself.'

Jack unclenched his fist, where the dice still lay. He closed his fingers around them and shook them even though they could not spin, and let them drop to the floor, his eyes fixed on the priest. Even after the dice had tumbled and come to rest, he continued to look at the other man as if it were on the priest's face that he would read the sign. Whatever he saw there caused him to retrieve the dice without seeing what they showed.

'We are leaving,' he said. 'If you will not point out the track to the highway, we shall find it ourselves.'

'Please yourself,' the priest said.

'Hey Maggie,' Jack said softly. 'Come on, Maggie. It's time to leave here. Wake up.' He shook her gently by the shoulder and slowly she came back from her dreaming and looked around her, frowning. He made her get up from the sofa and had to support her as her legs threatened to turn once more to sponge. He led her through the dark scullery and the darker dairy and into the stable, where he propped her against a rail while he readied the horses. Then they walked out into the chill moist air of a fog that still pressed closely around. He was sober again but she was not. He made her mount first. The dog snarled at his heels but he ignored it. The priest emerged from the stable and went to help him up.

'That won't be necessary,' Jack said. But the man walked round the horse, held the saddle to stop it slipping and rather roughly grabbed hold of Jack's coat to pull him on.

'Your liquor muddled my wits,' Jack said.
They rode off, leaving the priest and his dog by the door of the stable.

'What became of our slave, John French?' the priest said, looking out into the unfathomable fog. He was the fourth of the six.

Out of silence, silence. From rain only rain. From the four winds, the four seasons. From the seasons, the surge of spring, lifelong summers, leaf-fall, bitter winter. For Molly Thick a third boy, born on Christmas day. 'Call him Christian then, father, shall us?' Christian it was, but the gifts were withheld. Neither smiles nor chuckles nor the funny infant words. No 'Ma' or 'Da'. Da died. Molly struggled with two lads and a pale, grimly serious babe with white face and pink neck and no hair, big ears that heard everything and a mouth that said nothing, ever. My fault, Molly thought, because there are sins in everyone's lives, hers included. She tended him but she never could love him. She dressed him but found him ugly. Talked to him and got no reply. The two bigger brothers noised in the tiny cottage and tumbled in the fields but they could not tumble with Christian, for whom everything seemed of a deadly solemnity. They made a ring round him, though. Never hurting him, never insulting, never shouting. Fighting the boys that teased or called him names, protecting this thin sprig of silent solitude and making sure that whatever they knew he knew too. There was the two-class school at Buckland, but Christian never went. Christian Thick didn't appear on anybody's agenda. His name was written down once, at the beginning, in the big book at Buckland church where everyone but the gippoes figured, and after that not once more. He never held a pencil, never opened a book, not even for the pictures. Molly wasn't one for stories, so all the stories he got were the fragments in people's speech, and there was precious little of that on the wooded hills where Adrian and Anthony worked from boyhood and Christian alongside them.

He was quick and unerring with the billhook, splitting narrow staves from top to bottom with a single stroke. When they stripped trunks for poles or timber, he stripped one half while the brothers worked at the other half between them. Still there was no smile but in his dedication was a form of happiness. From the frost of dawn to the dark of dusk, Christian Thick laboured by his brothers in the woods. They had the brawn, but his were the finer skills. With the billhook he was deft, but it was the axe he loved. He sharpened all three axes, and the hooks too, but his own axe was feather-edged, murder sharp even in summer when there was little work for it to do. Except when he was asleep, Christian's axe lived on Christian's shoulder.

Woodland was his. Stipple of light and shade. Huge boughs steady against gravity. In summer, green crowns lifted. Every dusk, the magic creeping through on velvet feet. '*Oh yes*!' he would have cried, had he known to cry. He did not like towns, highways, inns, fancy dress, strangers: it was a long list, getting longer. Top-coats and top-hats, carriages with thin wooden wheels, the paraphernalia of women, the impudence of children, know-all town folk, parties, birthdays, and holidays. A blackbird singing from the apple tree before dawn was all he wanted of musicians and choirs. Sundays he walked alone on the hills, studying. He studied the form and movement of clouds, the relation of bud to petal, twig to branch, leaf to twig. Signs in the soils and the sands, for every slight sign recorded a happening. No tiny scratch or divot came there by itself; no wren landed on wet brimble but droplets of water fell to earth in tiny crumbled troughs.

He became the demon stalker. He found the straying horses and the lost lambs and once tracked the squire's bull bought all the way off in Hereford when it broke its tether and wandered nearly to the next county. Clem Rose's dog disappeared for a week and Christian found it in another village, keeping company with a bitch.

Sleep came hardly to Christian Thick. He walked out, moon or no moon. His feet learned the tracks, his eyes reckoned the intensity of shadows, his ears missed nothing of tumbled water, rabbit patter, owl swoop. He carried no lantern, stood aside from meeting or greeting, preferred the woodland where none but he would venture in the deep dark. He liked to stalk where they had laboured by day, to squat by the warm ashes of their fires and to move among the newly kempt thickets and sniff by night the scent of shaven bark and leaf-mould overturned. On his shoulder, his axe.

The Halloween fog was very dense, but there was nothing in wind or weather to make Christian afraid, only what there was in man, and he wandered through on the fringes of the fog above the marsh, liking the impenetrable quiet, the way that everything was swallowed and breathed up again older, indistinct, uncertain of itself. He moved slowly into the fog and slowly withdrew from it again, exploring its shifting frontier on the slopes.

He came to the causeway and was thrilled by how this familiar track was altered, curves and corners coming at him just created, as if no one had ever trod this way before and it came into being for his very step. He knew to keep his eyes narrowed like a cat, by seeing less to see more.

First he heard voices, and then the sound of horses slowly picking their way through the mire. He dropped to one knee, keenly listening. Two horses. Distance hard to judge even for him. Closer than they seemed along the causeway. He withdrew a few steps to the trunk of a great tree, feeling the bark and sniffing it to know its kind. Pressed against the oak he listened to the snorting of the horses and to the rhythmical thunk of the hooves on the soft sedge of the verge. He slipped quietly to the far side of the oak and stood there hardly breathing as horses and riders passed within a few paces. If he had leapt and danced the riders might have remained unaware of him so dense was the fog at that point. But it was not so with the horses who knew at once that a human creature stood by the tree and mistrusted it. The bay mare threw up her head and flashed the whites of her eyes, but the black filly reared and twisted and noised in her fright.

'Whoa there!' the man's voice called out. 'Whoa my pretty!' The filly quieted and the horses went on. At the foot of the oak tree lay the body of Maggie Fox. Christian Thick waited for the horses to stop and turn back but they did not. He came slowly forward to where the girl lay and when he bent over her, he could see the whiteness of her skin and hear the aspiration of her breath. He put out his hand and touched her face and something passed between the soft skin of her face and the pelt of his hand. He had not known that girls were made of subtly different stuff. In that instant, the heart of Christian Thick was full. He took off his jacket and covered her with it and with his arm he cradled her head so that it should not be damp and he wished to sing to her as she lay senseless but he could not sing. John French crept out of the fog, growling low and deep in his throat. Christian held out a hand towards the dog, but the dog growled on, backing slowly off before turning tail.

Christian Thick sat on by the side of the girl, waiting for her to come to. Now he wore no jacket but he was oblivious to the clammy cold. At last he heard something, got quickly to his feet and retreated into the fog. The dog trotted up, followed by the figure of the priest with his lantern.

'Show us what you've got, French,' the priest said. The priest crouched over the girl, putting down his light. The dog watched in Christian's direction, but the priest took no notice. He pulled the girl to a sitting position, lifted her up, wobbling as he stood upright, and reached for his lantern. Christian watched them leave, waited a few instants and followed. Twice the dog came back out of the fog, eyeing him, but ahead of them the priest walked on towards Urley House, bearing the girl over his shoulder. Later, Christian Thick crouched by the window of the back kitchen, peering into the dim room. He watched as the man who called him slave saw to the fire. He watched on as the man stood over the body of the girl stretched out on the settee. He felt the shape of something ugly in the room although he hardly knew what. He raised his arm and smashed a window pane with the elbow. As he ducked out of sight, he saw the priest straighten up and his eyes dart to the window.

Christian kept his vigil over Urley House, by this window or that. French shadowed him, growling, but the priest did not come out of the house. Later the girl was on her feet, and Christian saw her talking with the priest in the back kitchen, but he could not hear what was said. He heard the door of the stables open and he saw her stand bewildered outside the door before she went in. Later still, she had climbed the stairs with a lamp and after that she was lost to his view.

He watched the priest sitting by the fire in the back kitchen, toying with some small articles in his hand, then he quietly made his way to the stable and hid under his blanket on the straw. When he rose later, the priest was still by the fire and the small articles, one red and one white, lay on the stool in front of him. On the other stool was a root with the shape of a homunculus. One leg had been cut off, for the Mandragorite did not favour powders for his tea. He preferred a whole limb, stewed.

Chapter Four

He Upp'd His Sweet Martini-Henry

Aye, Hell was thick with captains. (Siegfried Sassoon)

COCKLER was the fifth of the six. He was from London, but he wasn't what Dorset folk thought of as a Lunn'ner, possessing neither wealth nor pretensions of wealth. At the time of his arrival in middle Dorset, Cockler had three ha'pence in his pocket, enough for a pint of ordinary. His material assets consisted of one elderly horse, one elderly covered wagon and a jumble of odd belongings, referred to collectively as his 'rig' and his 'stuff'. There were surprising items among the stuff, but not much of it was marketable. There was also a dog who was large and woolly and generally affable except towards rabbits. This dog was not what you'd usually term a rabbiter, being too big for warren work, but he was still lethal at close quarters and much quicker than he looked. Cockler's evening meal was normally rabbit, or occasionally hare. Sometimes pheasant, but these pheasants were grabbed from their roosts as a farmer might grab a roosting chicken, without help from the dog.

Cockler was slim and strong like wire. He was a lively dancer of reels and hornpipes and certain impish steps all his own, an acute observer, a lover of laughter and stories. He had a way with horses and women, and both were gentle ways. Cockler was clever with axles and gears and bearings. He was handy with levers and wrenches. He knew his way around a boat, its ropes and rigging. He was not a wealthy man as bankers know wealth, but bankers know wealth narrowly.

Cockler's camp that night of thick fog was on a broad verge not far from the church at Wootton and he and his horse and dog had had a long day of it, having plodded the breadth of the Blackmore Vale, all the way from Cranborne Chase, fifteen miles as the crow flies and double that by lane and track. They had spent the previous night at Handley, a chilly spot with little to recommend it in Cockler's eyes. He had drifted that way to avoid Shaftesbury — it was his habit to avoid towns — and discovered that Handley was a place to which a number of dubious types drifted, poachers and rustlers and smugglers, people who were as likely to poach and rustle from each other as from anyone else. If there was honour among thieves, not much of it was to be found in Handley, according to Cockler, and there was nothing much to poach because everything had been already poached. There was the depressing air of the dishevelled and the makeshift with which the luckless and lawless are surrounded. Outside the tumble-down houses had collected a litter of gateposts and wagon wheels and barrels and butts and basins that had once been other people's, the road was a dribble of chalk and rock between a chaos of potholes, the farms were no longer farmed, the chickens lacked a full complement of feathers and nobody appeared to own the dogs. Cockler would have continued on through, but was caught by a sudden storm and spent an uneasy night, attracting the attention of at least one prowler and a gang of skinny curs. His own dog crawled under the wagon and growled when anything came too close. Cockler slept above with his knobstick at his side.

The next night's campsite was very different, a pleasant meadow by a tidy village with the church spire rising comfortably overhead.

Cockler often chose the vicinity of churches to camp, not because he had any interest in their contents or wares but because crimes and confrontations seemed less likely to take place within their immediate orbit. People tended to remember their charitable side when over-looked by sacred tower or steeple, which for Cockler meant a degree or two less of suspicion and hostility and, sometimes, a chicken's egg or a mug of fresh milk.

Cockler's rig drew into the meadow in mid-afternoon, and leaving the dog to look after the horse and wagon its driver took a stroll over the fields and a bath in the brook, according to his daily custom. Cockler's baths were not for the sake of form. He had a scrubbing brush and a large brick of coal tar soap and these he employed with tremendous vigour. When Cockler came out of his bath, he came out pink and purged. Serious baths had been the rule in his father's house-hold, and Cockler insisted scrupulously on this rule since he had been on the road. Travellers bore various signs of their travels – sunburn and patched clothes and worn heels to their boots and caps that had taken on the shape of their owners' heads – but dirt was among the most frequent of these signs and this Cockler did not endure. During his ablutions, he scrubbed his body and washed his thick, curly hair and cleaned under his nails and finished up by shaving with the aid of a razor and a small mirror. He also laundered enough clothes to be sure of a clean shirt and trousers when he needed them.

Cockler was a traveller by necessity rather than by disposition, on his way to find a job. He had heard that there were jobs to be had in the Cornish tin mines, what with the miners gone to war, and Cockler was as competent with a pick or a pump as the next man, and maybe more so. He'd fought alongside Cornishmen at the front and enjoyed their forthright and humorous approach to things and the way they spoke of home. As a matter of fact, he had appreciated their manliness, and manliness was something Cockler found relaxing in a man, just as he enjoyed its correspondence in a woman. In his pocket he had the name of a man who managed a mine among the menhirs and dolmens of the Atlantic coast.

After his bath Cockler laid a fire and while it took he squatted behind his wagon and plucked a chicken he had come across in Handley. He did this discreetly, taking care to collect the feathers and add them to his fire so that no sign of a plucked chicken remained around his campsite. For he knew well that the sight of a traveller plucking a chicken caused passers-by to get anxious about their coops, an anxiety that Cockler treated as natural. He would have counted his own chickens had the positions been reversed.

The bird took a couple of hours to boil and Cockler wandered off to look for some greens to add to the pot, finding only a handful of coarse dandelions and a few old bulbs of wild garlic. His mother had gathered herbs by the Thames when he was a child. What he remembered best was the great nettle harvest of springtime when they would go down to the edge of the marshes and cut swathes of young nettle, eating some of it boiled as a green vegetable and drying the rest for tea. His father drank two cups of nettle tea every day of the year, and there wasn't a grey hair on his head on the day he died.

The fog began coming in about the time the meal was ready, and Cockler put a blanket round his shoulders as he ate. The dog got the bones and the skin and the innards and a bowl of the soup, too, but there was still plenty left for breakfast in the morning. The mare was free to crop the verges as she pleased. Cockler didn't tie her at night, it being understood that it was part of the dog's function to keep an eye on her if need be.

Shortly after dark, Cockler turned in and slept soundly until roused by the dog's growls and the sound of a man's voice.

'I've got a stick in my hand,' said Cockler, grabbing up his knobstick.

'Where are we?' said the man's voice.

'I don't know where the bleed you are, but I'm 'ere in the wagon, stick in hand, and if you'll just push on the way you were going, there's no bother to either of us.'

'Advance one and be recognised,' said the man.

'Advance be buggered,' said Cockler, crawling to the back of his wagon and lifting the canvas. 'What are you anyway, wandering about in the fog at dead of night?'

'Yeoman, Lance Corporal, Dorsetshire Regiment.'

'Not 'ere, you're not. We don't need no lance-corporals 'ere.'

'Where's your regiment, trenches, bivouac?'

Cockler threw on his coat and climbed down from his wagon. The fog was very thick. He walked over and kicked at what remained of his fire, which threw out a spray of sparks and grew red at its heart. He added a couple of sticks, squatted down and blew life into the flames.

'Are you off your rocker or what?' he demanded.

'I may be a little confused,' the soldier said.

'That's not confusion. It's confusion when you don't know whether it's rabbit or pheasant you ate last night. But if you reckon you're in the trenches in France when all the time you're somewhere between Middlemarsh and Buckland, then confusion doesn't do for it.'

'Upset and confused,' the soldier said, with a strange laugh.

'You'd best come up to this fire and warm up a bit, and I may even have a dram left over to bring a bit of warmth to your vitals.'

The sticks had caught and Cockler added a few more before pulling out a flask from the inside pocket of his coat and passing it to the man, who drank.

'This is not France,' he said.

'Too right it's not. This 'ere is Blighty, mate. Where you always wanted to be. This is the white cliffs and the green hills and whatnot. This is medals pinned on yer tit and speeches by the King and girls lining up to be first with the returning heroes. That's what this is.'

'They won't be pinning any medals on me,' the other said.

'Nor on me, mate. But we can get along without that, can't we. A bit of a fire and a flask with something in it and a chicken leg for tea goes a lot further than a tin trinket to my mind.'

'I have to go back,' the soldier said suddenly, getting up.

'Not tonight you don't, friend. Tomorrow maybe or next week or never if you take a leaf out of my book. You hang on where you are by the fire and take another tot of this and let 'em get on with things over there without you.'

'Not to France. To find Maggie.' The soldier turned away from the fire and looked wildly behind him into the ragged uniformity of the fog.

Cockler watched him. 'There's no point in rushing off into that, I can tell you,' he said. 'It's like fighting your own blanket out there.'

The soldier began cursing the war and the generals and the King as well and then cursed himself. 'It's the priest that's got the dice!' he said suddenly, and Cockler thought he'd gone off again to the trenches or to some other netherland.

'Stick to the point,' Cockler said. 'The point is that you did what any sensible feller would do and got out of the great fuck-up. That's what we called it after Loos, the Great Fuck-Up. I even heard officers call it that. But they had a part in it, or some of them. One morning the wind was wrong but the silly buggers were still setting off the gas and it came drifting back into our own trenches. I thought, well I'm not bloody having this and I went up to the officers with the canisters and told 'em to switch the stuff off. The *accessory*, they called it. I'll give them bloody accessory. They could see with their own eyes where it was going, but all they was interested in was me speaking out of turn, me being a mere lance-corporal like yerself. I knew one of 'em any-way, a pugnacious little twerp with two pips up, and he was going on about how "the programme must be carried out whatever the condi-tions" and this programme of his was the root of the whole cock-up, as if we weren't real people and the enemy didn't have a mind and a life wasn't a life, but some redtab fancied a programme which meant firing gas into a headwind and poisoning yer own people. He was waving a piece of paper at me, and I told him to give it over so that I could stick it up 'is backside, so he got nasty then and drew his pistol on me.'

'He arrested you?' The soldier was squatting opposite him across the fire.

'No 'e didn't. Because I shot him.'

65

'You shot an officer?'

'Too true I did. I upp'd me sweet Martini 'Enry and put a ball through his leg. I never 'ad a moment's regret about it neither. I'd do the same again. It got me out of the war and it stopped him right enough.'

'There was another one there, you said.'

'The other one run off, to get 'elp maybe, and I wasn't there when he got back. I made myself scarce as they say. I was back in Bethan before dark. On the way, there was two cats feeding on a corpse. I walked the canal by night then slept up in Lily I think it was. I reckoned I'd learned one thing from all that which was getting around by dark without a light. I couldn't stick the dark when I was young. Maybe comes of being a city boy. There's always a light in the city somewhere or a glow in the sky at least. But I've got to like it now, that great reach of black above you, like God in an admiral's hat. 'Course I never saw it real black until I got back 'ere and set off with the wagon. The wagon was me grandpa Cockler's and he used it for the cockles. You can still smell 'em, I reckon, although it could be imagination because that's a fair while ago. The cockling, I mean.'

'Cockling?'

'Cockles. Me grandfather worked the Thames flats down by Thurrock and 'is grandfather before him and I reckon a good way further back too since it's 'ow we got our name.'

'Your name's Cockle?'

'Cockler. With a ''r'' at the tail. Me father would've gone into it too but the cockles were givin' out because of something they were doin' to the river, so me grandfather said, and he should know. Another one of their programmes I shouldn't wonder. Me father moved to London and took up with bicycles instead, which was cleaner work he said and shorter hours. But I went out with me grandfather when I was a lad, and I liked it out there with the gulls and the sand ribbed like a whale and the river going on by. Still, me grandfather died and I worked with me father on the bicycles after that until the war came along.'

'Why did you sign up?'

'It all looked a bit different when you saw it from then.'

'How did you get back to England?'

'I don't want to go into all that.'

'If you don't, you don't. But maybe you do, after all,' said the soldier.

Cockler laughed. 'What are you, chaplain or croaker?' he said.

'Croaker?'

'One of them that turns up when you're about to croak.'

'Tell me the story,' the soldier said.

'I will then. You've got me out of bed and me sleep's gone and maybe the fire and the fog's about right for ... for things that seem a continent ago and moons away, like they happened in a different world almost. I was in Lily. I wasn't in a hurry to go near where there was uniforms and there was uniforms all over, and where there's uniforms there's queues and questions and bits of paper. I got a train to the coast but I travelled in the cab with the driver, who was French of course. Cost me a pack of cigarettes. After that I kept pushing up along the coast going east and north using the night for moving and the days to hole up, and I kept as close to the sea as I could. I had a bit of biscuit and bully which was meant for the attack and it kept me goin' near enough. It was like leaving the circus those nights walking by the black water with flares in the sky to the south and the rumble of the guns at dawn and beyond them of other guns and of more guns beyond them. I went through the lines one night by the light of the moon, the Belgian and the German all in one go, and somebody might've shot me then but there wasn't a lot goin' on up there compared to where we were. They were leavin' each other pretty much alone was my feeling, especially hard up by the sea. Most likely the sea made 'em all feel a bit less important and they couldn't set their minds on killin' so well. The German trenches just sputtered out in some dunes, suddenly there was nothing, not a jerry can or a spent shell or the whiff of a latrine. It was light by then and the gunfire had started up somewhere behind me but I was out of it so I went for a swim to wash some of it out of me hair and there was another bloke swimming there who could 'ave been German or Belgian or neither, could've been the Kaiser for that matter, but we didn't give a monkey's, we just waved to each other and got on with it, both of us in our birthday suits. What I needed was something to wear that wasn't a uniform so I 'ad to help myself to that from a farmhouse where nobody was around and I left me rifle and some of me kit there as a swap. I took a bit o' bread and cheese as well, which I didn't much like to do, but I was gettin' hungry. So I left me bowie knife too. Then I came into Ostend which is a proper sort of place with a fishing fleet and a higgle of houses by the sea and a fish market and plenty of boats.'

Cockler fell silent, thinking of the fish market at Ostend and the white boat and the girl.

'Go on,' said the soldier.

'I went down to the market to have a look at what they caught there, and what I saw was a lot of cockles, big black ones. There was mussels and whelks and crabs and that, but the cockles were the best I'd ever seen, which seemed like a sign somehow, me being a Cockler. Soon as I saw 'em, I thought to myself, here's where I get my ticket to Blighty. And it was when I was staring at those big cockles that the girl who was selling 'em spoke to me. I didn't understand a word of the lingo but I've got hands and eyes and what with one thing and another it was as easy as pie to get on with that girl, and a man would have to be a fool not to, to my way of thinking, her being what she was. I was lucky that I'd just had a wash and found a clean shirt and pair of trousers and didn't smell of nothing but the sea. I asked her for a job straight out. All I had to do was to mime picking a few cockles and she got it right away and yes she said. *Oui*, she went, that would be OK and we fixed to meet the next morning. I got the time because she made the shape of the sun comin' up, and the sun did come up when she did that. It was like she was holding it in front of her face.'

Cockler thought of her with the sun in her arms.

'I never had a girl,' the soldier said, staring into the fire.

'What, *never*?'

'They make me nervous,' Jack said. 'Like they were another race. Like they go about in a bubble of a different kind of air.'

'There ain't no bubble 'cept one you been blowing yerself,' Cockler said. 'I bet you went to one of them posh schools. You speak like a toff anyway, though I don't mean no harm by saying it. How come they didn't make you an officer?'

'They told me I could take officer training but I said no. My brother was an officer, and I didn't like what it did to him. You're right about the school, though.'

'There you are then. That sort o' place do specialise in bubble-blowing.'

'Go on,' the soldier said.

'Her name was Anouk and her bloke was killed at the front almost as soon as he got there. Her father was dead too, and her mother had moved out into the country when the war got going and she stayed by 'erself with the cockle business, I reckon because it was all that was left of what used to be. She had his photo by her bed and never moved it all the time I was with her and I used to see her looking at it sometimes but it didn't make no difference to me. I liked her better for going on loving him at the same time she was loving me. Her heart was as big as an orchard and there was room there for more than one. But she told me I was better at the cockles than he was. Seems he was a bit of a dreamer and got to thinking about other things, but I'm not like that. If I'm picking cockles my mind's on cockles and I always wanted to get more in than her, and even though she was quicker'n me at the beginning, I soon caught up and we was a good team all things considered, on the beach and in the boat and everywhere. I would've stayed there papers or no papers. They got to know me at the market and the harbour, and they knew I was English and they didn't give a damn about that. I was a seaman like themselves is the way they saw it and seamen most places have a way of sticking together, maybe because they all know what it means when a storm blows up sudden. Which is what 'appened to us when we were coming back from the cockles.'

He got up and fetched a few more pieces of wood from over by the wagon and fed them to the fire, which was doing all right without them.

'The best cockles were on a spit of land that ran out into a narrow point a mile or two down the coast and we'd go there in her boat. It wasn't no more than a skiff with a sail, and when we was loaded there was only a couple of inches between the water and gunnel. The wind was gen'rally against us going back to the harbour so there wasn't much room for error. Well it was a sheltered stretch of water, but it made you think once or twice when the clouds boiled up and if we didn't like the look of the sky, we'd keep in close to the shore of the bay. But that partic'lar day, we was on the way out with only the empty boxes and there was no warning. It just blew up out of nothing. The rumble of guns was louder that morning and I remember wonderin' whether it was our lot or theirs going over the top, and now when I think of it, it's like those bleedin' guns started something off that wouldn't have started, because there was nothing in the sky to tell you what was going to happen. There was a pink dawn in front and pale yellow behind and only a few clouds scudding about in no hurry and the sea was smooth and easy with just a slight swell coming from behind us and tipping us fore and aft in a pleasant kind of way.'

'She died,' said the soldier.

'The mast must've smacked 'er as we went over. I thought at first she was trapped underneath, but it wasn't that or she would have been there later. It was the mast just came down on top of her. There was a thud that might have been something else, but it wasn't. I swam about like a madman and I dived until the water was coming out of my ears,

71

but the storm was carrying me away all the time and I never saw a sign of Anouk. She was wearing her red jersey that morning. I liked that red jersey because it went with the red stripe round the boat, and it went with her face too. That wasn't 'ard because everything went with her face. But specially that red jersey. She looked like the sun in a red sunrise is what, and if I live out my years, which I won't to be sure, I'll never see anything so fine as she was sitting in that white boat with all the sea and the sky.'

Tears glinted in the firelight on his face, but he let them be as if they didn't belong to him.

'I didn't care whether I lived or died, or so I thought, and I don't know what the bleed it is that keeps a man hanging on to his little bit of life but the hull came by and I clung on to it. Maybe I still thought she might have made it to the beach, but I'd heard the thud and I knew really that she'd gone. They couldn't find her body, not that day nor afterwards. The boat was washed up on the beach, and me with it, but the storm blew itself out as quick as it'd come, and there wasn't much wrong with the boat nor with me neither. I hung around for a few days and fixed up the boat there on the beach and some of the fishermen came and said something to me, gave me food and that, and one of them brought me a big waterproof because he knew what I was planning, which didn't take much gumption being as I was fixing the skiff and sleeping on the beach. Next day he came along with a few tools and a couple of planks and a needle and some cord for the sail and we secured the mast and patched up the rudder where it was broke and sewed up the sails. In the evening I sat there and watched out over the water for something red in the waves but in fact I didn't want to know what the sea had done to her. That night I set out, because the wind had swung to the east and I thought it was strong enough to take me over in one night, which it did right enough, not that I cared much. I sunk the boat close into the shore because I didn't want to look on its white hull and its red stripe any more, then I swam in and it was Kent.'

He was silent a moment before going on.

'So you see the shooting of the officer is nothing to me, and all the bodies I saw dead were nothing next to the body I didn't see dead, which is a pitiful thought but a true one because the war went away when I met her, and it'll go away for you too, Johnny, if you find something to cling on to and a reason to cling on to it.'

'Jack. My name's Jack.'

'Short for John but.'

'Nobody calls me John.'

'I'll be the first then, Johnny me lad. Me grandfather was John and they all called him Johnny. There's plenty of folk in Thurrock and Stifford remember Johnny Cockler.'

'What's your own name?'

'You know what, I don't bother with it no more. Just Cockler'll do. Maybe it was the army that did it to me. Cockler this and Cockler that. Cockler come and Cockler go. On the forms you always had to put your first name last as if it were a kind of bleedin' afterthought. So I did away with it.'

'That was the war.'

'I'm still at war, mate,' Cockler said.

Chapter Five

The Just Builder

There's still a place in the line for you! (Recruitment poster, 1915)

EARLY on the morning of Halloween, a dense pall of fog lay along the Cerne and the Piddle, and only the tops of the hills that overlooked the valleys stood clear in the morning light. Slowly the fog retreated down the slopes to gather sullenly in the deeper parts of the valleys and to lie up in thick coils over the surfaces of the rivers and over all the extent of the marshland it loved.

Bill Bate was afoot when the fog was still thick. The kettle boiled on the hob, rashers of bacon sizzled in the pan. You could feed on the smell alone, he thought. Black tea, very sweet, and the smell of bacon getting crisp. Fat spat on the hotplate. Diced horse mushroom added to the pan. The smell sweetened. Four thick slices of bread face down to toast. A pair of eggs to fry when the mushrooms were out and the bacon beginning to brown. A second cup of tea, with more sugar this time. Coat by the door. Walking boots ready on the doormat. Stalker's hat awaiting the stalker. He took his breakfast slowly, making it last. Had a slab of cheese with the third and fourth slice. On top of the cheese, a spoonful of honey, like his mother had. Before leaving, he made a couple of sandwiches, expecting a long day.

Bill Bate was a builder and what he liked most to build was stone. The best days of his life were when the horsecart came to the site on the first morning and he and the carter threw the stone down off the bed of the cart. He loved the rough feel of the stuff against his fingers,

74

the hollow thud as the big rocks hit the ground, the slight spray of chips as one rock hit another. Already on that first morning, his eye would light on the finest of the stones, choosing cornerstones, a lintel, a slab for the threshold. He had few tools and they were worn, but he didn't care for that. His best tools were his big capable hands. He would toss a huge rock in his hands, looking for the best face. He would lower one into place as if he were handling a small child. His houses were just. Just the right amount of mortar, a just balance between big stones and small, doors and windows, walls and roofs. He built everything from foundations up. His carpentry was bold and strong, without airs. He worked with a bag of six-inch nails, which plunged into the wood, whether sweet chestnut or oak or elm, as if scared by the hammer that drove them.

Some summer evenings he would walk to Milton to look at the abbey and people had seen him on his knees before it. Not before God but before the might and beauty of the building. It was a colossal work, inch perfect. He would spend hours at a time in studying it, how this had been done and how this. Inside, the heavy candelabra and the severe lines of pews and the pretension of the carved pulpit got in the way of the immense grandeur of the columns. But still the stone vaulting and tracery was something to marvel at, and he could have built such things, he felt, if he had lived in another age or in another place.

The war when it came had been sent for people like him. The news that the British Empire had declared war on Germany reached Cerne on Saturday 4 August 1914, and it was said that this was the only news that needed no more than twenty-four hours to reach every part of the kingdom, because it travelled with every bus, with every bicycle, on every footpath. The news of the old King's death might have been held up here and there through forgetfulness or indifference, but the war belonged at once to all of them. Within days, vehicles were being commandeered and trains were re-routed and horses were rounded up from stables and farms to be collected at the barracks. Dorchester became for a while the front line almost and Dorchester railway station like a Waterloo.

But the war that might have been the making of Bill Bate nearly destroyed him. When they turned him down at the recruiting office in Dorchester, he could not go home that night. He drank himself into a fury in *The Three Mariners* on Broad Street and picked a fight with a group of soldiers from the barracks. There were five of them less drunk than he was, and they dragged him into the courtyard and might have killed him there because he would not stop getting up after they hit him. He wanted them to kill him. He urged them repeatedly to do so, until at last they left him there, on his feet, shouting taunts at them as they disappeared. He would have made a good soldier. He was sure of it, although he never said so aloud. He wanted to fight for his country because his country was the finest place of his imagining. All around, the seas, and beyond the seas, the other. The island of Britain was something perfect, made of wooded hills and leafy lanes, chalk pits and stone quarries, farmyards and village greens, stone walls and stone wells. Water everywhere, in rivers, ponds, lakes, streams, brooks, lochs, canals. A place where the world and its animals would never go thirsty.

'Yes, dammit,' he shouted aloud to an imaginary antagonist that night after leaving *The Giant's Club*. 'Yes, dammit,' he repeated to himself as he sat alone at his kitchen table in the dark. This land was the fairest of all, worth giving your life for, despite the peacocking politicians. He'd seen Lloyd George once, getting out of a motor car by *The Digby Hotel* in Sherborne, passing through on his way west. The man was short, with long hair and a dapper style. This was not an eagle, but more like a wagtail. There was too much charm and not enough claw. Clever he might be, but this was not a fit leader for a great land. And the King? Bill Bate had no illusions about George the Fifth. Royal pomp and circumstance were an irrelevance to what Bate thought of his native land, his native tongue, his people. It was not kings and queens he respected but something much older and finer than all of them.

If a man didn't fight, Bate thought, he was like the start of a crack in the masonry. He might be no more than a crumb of gravel in a film of mortar, but great stones are set on the delicate positioning of the small, he knew. That Saturday morning, he planned to start his day with a word in the squire's ear. He was known to Mr Clive Lawrence well enough, having built the great stone hay barn for him, and put up a cowshed to last a hundred years and re-faced the stables courtyard and made himself useful in other various ways. The squire might have heard of this Captain Yeoman, for he knew most of the families in the vicinity who counted. For sure he would appreciate at once the danger of a man speechifying against the war. The squire had stayed at home on account of his responsibilities as landlord and Justice of the Peace and colonel of the local militia, and Bate had stayed on account of a missing finger, but they were both men to do what they could for the greater cause.

A mile short of Minterne, Bate came on the Zenith left carelessly by the roadside. He kicked the start lever two or three times before satisfying himself that the motorcycle wasn't going anywhere unless it was pushed, and when he continued it was with a sharper step. They'd not have gone far on foot in the dark.

The interview with the squire was brief. Clive Lawrence learnt of the deserter and his speech and the abandoned motorbike, and Bate learnt of the stolen horses.

'His name's Jack Yeoman,' Bate said, 'and there's a brother who's a captain. You may know where they hail from, Mr Lawrence.'

'There are Yeomans with property in Somerset, near Taunton. I don't know of any closer than that.'

'I'll go after them,' Bill Bate said.

'Even you'll not catch them on foot, Bate. I've sent word to the police in Sherborne and Dorchester. We'll get news of my horses before too long.'

'I'm booted and spurred and I've got nought pending,' said Bate. 'There was a thick fog in the valleys all last night and it's hardly cleared yet. They took no saddles or bridles, you said. The ground's soft and the tracks will be clear enough. You go ahead with your enquiries, Mr Lawrence, and I'll just step out after them a short way. I'll let you know later if there's anything to report.'

'You're a good man, Bill Bate,' said the squire.

'Good doesn't come into it,' Bate said. 'There's a war on and they didn't see fit to let me in on the fighting, so I must do what I can. I don't like the idea of a man going round these parts spreading the stench of defeat and it's no more than my duty to lay my hands on

78

him. If he's gone back to Taunton or wherever, then that's beyond my reach, but if he's still on my beat, I'll be the one to find him, mark my words.'

'I don't doubt it,' Clive Lawrence said.

The fog still lurked on the lower slopes, but the horses' tracks were clear and deep over the meadow by the river bank. Two sets, one larger than the other. He bent down and measured the span of the larger hoofprint between thumb and middle finger. Then the smaller print, which was half-an-inch narrower. He knew the horses. They shouldn't have been in the barn. The weather was mild and they should have been out still. The squire mollycoddling that black filly he boasted of. Irish blood he said, but Bate thought it a little on the spindly side. It might have speed but not over any distance. The other was a bay mare and Bate knew that one too. The track led up the river then uphill out of the fog. He could see where they had galloped, where cantered, where trotted. He found where they had stopped on the ridge and where they had got lost in the wood. He tracked them downhill off Minterne Ridge heading towards Dogbury and when he came to the pinewoods by Lyon Gate where the woodcutters were working, it was not yet eight o'clock. In a clearing in the woods, he came upon Adrian and Anthony Thick. Bate knew these men for they would sometimes dress stone for him when it was neither the season for timber to be felled nor hedges to be hedged nor trees to be pruned. Their younger brother Christian Thick would not dress stone, nor even carry it, keeping a little way apart, cutting shoots for hurdles or splitting faggots with deadly aim. Runaway horses belonging to the squire, Bill Bate told them.

'They horses have riders,' said Adrian, inspecting the prints. 'If Christian were about, he'd likely know about the riders as well. There's nobody reads a trail better'n what Christian do. They'm not runaways, they'm stolen.'

''Tis all the same to me,' said Bill Bate squaring his shoulders, and after he went on the brothers agreed that whoever had taken the horses had better watch out.

Ahead of Bate was the marshland now, and the fog came swiftly back, threaded through the trees, muffling and deluding. Bate liked all weathers, strong winds and fair days and even the long grey drizzles when the clouds would sit tight against the hilltops like a besieging enemy interminably encamped. Suchlike was good working weather, Bate said, there were no distractions for god or man. He worked to keep off the melancholy then, labouring with the heavy stones through hours at a stretch, exhausting those he took on to split and dress the stone until he was doing half their job as well, working with a kind of ferocity as if the world wouldn't last long enough for the building of what he had to build. There was something of that mood in him now as he plunged into the fog following the hoofprints.

He had to watch his own step hereabouts and the fog lay so thick that he needed to stoop to see the prints, deep and sharp though they were in the oozing turf. Extraordinary sureness of the animals who'd picked their way along these narrow paths with inches separating the edge of the hoof from the lip of the mire. The ends of fallen branches black with wet stood up from the bog like the arms of the drowning, and Bate had a sudden vision of what the deserter had deserted, a cemetery of sunken hope. It shocked him, because this was far from his own image of Belgian battlefields with the grand thunder of the big guns and the brave charges. But had there not been one photograph in the *War News*, one that had escaped the editor's eye, a misted land of pools and dead trees, that told of something other than glory?

Bate dismissed it with a shake of the head and went on. Here in a clearing the horses had stopped once more, the half circles of the horseshoes scored in jumbled patterns over the soft turf, and beside them precise and definite the prints of a man's boots, not walking but standing in front of the horses where they had shuffled and stamped. Around the man's prints, the petalled pawmarks of a dog. Then all of them, man, dog and horses had moved off together, it seemed, and so Bill Bate came to the house on the marsh in the muffling fog.

He dropped to one knee at the entrance to the yard, where a criss-cross of hoofprints showed in the mud. On the causeway, the prints told him that the horses had left and come back and, probably, left again. In the stable he saw fresh droppings and a few damp husks of grain left in the bottom of the manger and so he went into the house, knocking at the door and calling out but expecting no one and finding the same. In the back kitchen, the fire was out but the teapot was still hot. Whoever owned the house had gone too it seemed, so maybe the girl and the boy were on one horse, or even there was a third horse, although he did not think so. All this Bate pondered methodically, building the possibilities, of which there seemed to be two: the person who lived here was known to them or they had arrived by chance and he had decided to help them out. He might have learned more from going upstairs but he did not do so out of his country manners which said that a man's kitchen in his absence might on occasion be entered

81

but that the rooms upstairs were off limits. He followed the causeway to the main road and here he found hoofprints heading south, but it would be the devil's own job to track them on that stony surface and if he missed the way he could be off on a wild goose chase. All things considered he preferred to go back to the house and wait there awhile. He felt more comfortable doing his waiting outside, preferring the open air over his head and the good earth underfoot. Preferring also to walk than to stand, he strolled in the vicinity of Urley Moor observing the fog growing thin as the day warmed, and exploring the pathways through the mire. His eye was fond of leaf and moss and all things green. Pools were as thrilling to him almost as when he had first splashed into a puddle aged near nought, knowing it to be a live thing. It was later that he learned the curious word it had on it, *puddle*, a wet and muddy word sure enough, and later still when he learned how a word created the illusion that the object it described was everywhere the same. He kept to his boy's eye view of things, which said that every puddle was different, and every pool contained secrets of a different kind.

He was gazing into one such pool wondering whether the tiny air bubbles were caused by eel or loach or merely some slight vegetative movement in the mud when he heard the clopping of hooves along the track and the creaking of a cart's wooden wheels. He strode back to the yard to find that the cart had stopped out of sight. He kept hidden and watched, and there coming round the corner was the deserter, without horse or bag, just himself hurrying towards the house looking up at the windows and going straight to the stable door. He disappeared inside without knocking or calling out. Bate heard the wagon turning on the causeway and glimpsed patches of its white canopy flitting off behind the line of trees.

He walked up to the stable door and waited there, listening. When he heard the inner door swing open, he swiftly entered the stable as Jack was about to come out, appearing suddenly at the doorway, and standing there with his arms crossed over his chest.

'You came after me,' Jack Yeoman said.

'That's right,' said Bill Bate.

'So now you've found me. What do you want?'

'To deliver your hide to Dorchester barracks. No more 'n that.'

'It's none of your business.'

'I've made it my business.'

'You don't understand what you're dealing with.'

'But I do, sonny. There's a war being lost and there's people not fighting. It's that simple.'

'It's not *a* war.'

'I don't expect it to be pretty. There's plenty of folk dying, and plenty more getting dirty. But if people won't do their duty then we've lost more than a war, we've lost the lot.'

'Just what *lot* are you talking about?'

'You don't need me to spell it out for you. Duty's at the heart of it all.'

'I've no time to listen to this.'

'Make time. I'm here in the doorway and I'm not budging.' He was framed against the light coming through the doorway, broad as a boulder.

'Duty to *what*, I want to know,' Jack said.

'Duty to your country. To this land.'

'You can't be dutiful to a piece of earth. You can love it maybe but it doesn't tell you what to do.'

'You know what I mean.'

'No I don't. A country's just land and land's just earth and rock.'

'Nation, then. Stop fiddling with words.'

'Nation's not just a word, it's a system. It's got a top and a bottom, with government and laws.'

'I'm not talking about duty to a government and a book of rules. Governments change. A country doesn't.'

'This war is not fought for the country.'

'What the bloody hell is it fought for then?'

'It's fought for the handful of people who own everything and the bigger handful who help them keep it. Not for the miners but for the mine owners. Not for the shopkeepers but for the banks. Not for the ordinary people who live in small homes and dig their gardens on a Sunday but for the shipping companies and the law firms who work for them. If the war gets won, it's the rich and the powerful who win. If it's lost, they'll be the first to find a way out. The rest lose whatever happens.'

'Don't you preach to me, sonny. I've heard all this guff before and it don't accord with my way of thinking. A man's got a place and that's where his duty lies. It's not everybody that's born a king and if people get to wondering ''why not?'' then you've got passengers thinking themselves coachmen or a carriage taking itself for a horse.'

'When the horse is out of control and the coachman's fallen off, it's the people in the carriage that must do something about it. If you'd seen what it's like out there, you couldn't think like you do. It's a world gone mad. It's something that God never intended, like angels burning and children starving and cemeteries torn up. And there's people behind it counting their money and measuring their fame and possessions and relying on people like you to do their dirty work for them.'

'You're an envious little bugger is what you are.'

Jack Yeoman went to leave then, walking up to Bate and when the man didn't move trying to shoulder him out of the way but Bate didn't shift any more than a wall, so Jack took a swing at him. Bate let the blow smack against his jaw then caught hold of the arm and twisted it downwards so Jack stumbled backwards against the doorpost then Bate's other forearm came flat across his throat under his chin. Jack swung with his free arm but it did hardly more than slap the man on the back and Bate chuckled.

'You'll have to do better than that, sonny,' he said, and he seized the boy by his shoulders and flung him to the floor of the stable with a twisting movement of his torso. Then he stepped back into the doorway as before.

'You'll have to do a lot better than that,' he said.

Jack got up crouching and hurled himself at the man's legs and his momentum and bulk caught Bate by surprise so he couldn't stop himself toppling backwards, his arms flailing out to catch hold of the doorjambs but missing. Jack was first to his feet but Bate flipped out one arm from the deck as the boy shot past and grabbed hold of his ankle. Then Jack swivelled and kicked him on the side of the face. No more chuckling now. Jack might have run for it and got as far as the house, but the kick in the face was the red rag, and if the fight didn't end now it would go on later that day or the next day or until the finish because there was no mistaking what manner of man was Bill Bate when the red rag was out. He was born under the sign of the bull and lived under it, too, not a foolish bull by any means but a bull still, with its strength and bloody-mindedness.

Jack stayed where he was while Bate got up and they squared up to each other like prizefighters. Bate advanced and Jack punched him twice on the cheek with his long left arm but Bate ignored the jabs and came steadily on until he was close enough to reach up and get one arm round the boy's neck, with the other completing the headlock. Then he squeezed. Jack's face turned red and he started to choke and Bate watched him coolly before dropping him like a stone and standing back.

'You'll have to do better than that,' said Bill Bate. But his cheekbone smarted from the jabs and under the eye the swelling had started, like something stirring.

Jack's breath wouldn't come back and his sense had gone with it and when the first came back it was without the other. He got to his feet, came forward, fists up, but Bate's anger was gone and he wouldn't fight him any more.

'I can do that again and you know it,' he said, 'but it wouldn't prove anything. We'll go back to Cerne now, you and I, and there's a coach to Dorchester at noon and you can be back in the army by tea-time.'

'Might as well finish me,' Jack panted, coming forward. 'I'm not going back.'

Bate fended him off.

'I'm not giving you a choice,' he said.

'First let me find Maggie Fox at least.'

'Your girl? She's no concern of mine.'

'From Dorchester, they'll take me away. There'll be a court martial somewhere. The army doesn't bother informing grieving relatives. I brought Maggie with me and I must find her. After that, I'll come with you to the barracks. You have my word.'

'What value should I put on the word of a deserter?'

'Take my word or finish the fight.'

Bate deliberated. This way he might get hold of the horses as well and return them to the squire on the way back to Cerne.

'You must shake on it,' he said. 'But watch out if you don't mean to stick by your word. Or next time I squeeze your hand, it'll be to crush it.'

Jack shook the hefty hand that was offered him.

'What have you done with your girl, then?' Bate said.

'There's a priest lives here,' Jack said. 'He must know.'

'Priest? There's no priest in Middlemarsh. Nearest one to here is Holnest, I reckon.'

'A priest of a kind. With a black and white sheepdog.'

'Maybe I have heard tell. But he's not here now. And the girl neither. How come you left her here on her own?'

'The fog was thick. She must have fallen from the horse. I lost her. Then I lost the horses. I was out there wandering about like a blind man.'

'I followed the prints of horses to the highway,' Bate said. 'They turned south. Back towards Minterne, or Buckland.' He gestured. 'I thought you were on one of them horses, but I didn't fancy tracking them along the highway.'

'She'll have gone to Hammond,' Jack said, 'to look for me.'

'We'll make for Hammond then,' said Bill Bate, 'but I'll eat my dinner first.'

He settled himself on a stone by the gate and started on his bread and cheese without offering any to the deserter.

Chapter Six

Peculiar Politeness of Hammond

He visualized the whole earthly solidity of this fragment of the West Country, this segment of astronomical clay from Glastonbury to Melbury Bubb... 'It is a God!' he cried in his heart.

(John Cowper Powys)

LOUIS YEOMAN bought the labourer's cottage in Hammond after his wife died in 1906 and furnished it with an old settee, an armchair, a desk, a bed, and a brassbound trunk full of books and pictures. His hermitage, he called it, and he would spend a day there, or sometimes two, alone with his books and his thoughts. As the children grew up, the length and frequency of these visits increased and, imperceptibly, his hermitage became his home. Charles ran the farm at Manston – 'Better than I ever did,' Louis said – and Jack boarded at Sherborne School. It was Maggie who missed Louis most. She would ride over to spend the day with him, and together they would walk on Bulbarrow Hill or stroll through the woods at Melcombe.

In truth, Hammond was a suitable place for a hermit. There were folk who lived at hidden Hammond who got lost on their way home, so they said in neighbouring villages, and visitors on horse and foot who turned back without ever arriving. In fact, it occupied a prominent enough position: a low flat hilltop clearly visible from Hazelbury. A rook launching itself from Rawlsbury Camp might settle on the tower of Hammond church with hardly a flap of its wings. But at night, or at dusk or in the driving rain or the snow, Hammond concealed itself within a maze of deceptively shaped woodlands and among pathways which led only to other pathways and tracks that shot right past to other places.

For most of a decade, Louis lived in his Hammond cottage, which he called Sophoula, meaning a little wisdom or perhaps it was the diminutive of Sophia, his wife's name. There was some talk locally about why a man with a big house and children should go off and live on his own, but this was affable enough talk in the main, and Hammond had a reputation as an affable sort of place, with a touch of the elfin. The entire area between Bulbarrow in the east and the Cerne Giant in the west, between Piddletrenthide in the south and Dungeon Hill in the north, had about it an element of faerie, naturally enough, for this was a remote place occult from the highways and market towns, and still largely immune from articles of trade and instruments of change. It was a medieval place, at a time when the Middle Ages were said to have been obliterated hundreds of years before. 'The Middle Ages *obliterated*!' Louis had exclaimed indignantly when he came across this expression. 'It takes more than a wretched dose of so-called humanism and a few technical novelties to obliterate the only true civilisation that Europe has known for a thousand years!' No doubt he was right in this, as far as the rural areas of middle Dorset were concerned. According to Louis, the elements of faerie were not in the least uniform. In his journal, he wrote:

If Hammond is touched by the elfin, then Middlemarsh, five miles away, is goblinesque. There's something druidical about Bulbarrow and Rawlsbury and nothing at all druidical about Plush or Ansty, which are down-to-earth sort of places with not much more magic than is to be found in the scent of a flower or the hum of a bumblebee. Dungeon Hill, as its name suggests, has a dark and violent past, connected with conflicts and terrors of the Bronze Age, and the shadow of this falls over Duntish. Buckland is a pleasant and auspicious sort of place, and the pixies are friendly thereabouts. As for Cerne Abbas, there is a feeling that all the humours have gathered here under the sign of the Giant, all the psychic states have left their traces, elfin, goblin, druid and warrior mage, yes, all the conditions and inspirations of man have met here in one age or another, which is doubtless the reason for the ancient story of St Augustine's blessing of the spring at the foot of Giant Hill with the splendid proclamation: *Cerno Deum*!

Since the day of Louis's funeral at Hammond church, the labourer's cottage called Sophoula had remained unopened and unvisited, quiet, as they say, as the grave. One month later, near enough, about mid-morning, a rider approached the village from the north, a girl on a slender black filly no more than two years old, with a second horse, larger and squarer following unridden behind. The girl rode easily but she looked anxiously towards the village as she went on.

The village appeared empty as she rode between the houses. It wore an air of peculiar politeness, as if no one ever raised their voices here, as if the walls of the low-roofed cottages were thick enough to hush all sounds of occupation, as if here cows would come and go without cowherds, birthdays without parties and whole centuries slide by without the whiff of want or war.

Maggie Fox knew at once that Jack was not at the cottage. There would have been some sign of her big noisy lad with raven-black hair who didn't know how to keep his voice down. She tied the horses to a tree by the gate and tried the front door, which they'd always pushed open without knocking because Louis said there was no need for that. But the door was locked. She looked in at the window of the front room where the curtain was half drawn and saw that everything on the window-shelf was as it always was, a pile of letters, two large lexicons, one Sanskrit and one ancient Greek, a book with a black leather bookmark. She tried to see which book he had been reading in the days before his death, but the title was turned away. She went round the house to the back door, which was unlocked. She stood for a moment in the silence of the tiny kitchen. On the shelves stood a green teapot and three green teacups, one of them cracked. She smiled to see it. When there were three of them for tea, Louis always took the cup with the crack. Next to the teapot was a biscuit tin, a sugar pot, one soup bowl and a few plates. How much of Louis's character was in these few unremarkable objects! How much of his dislike of formality and the simple economy of his life.

She went through into the front room where lived his settee, his single armchair and his books. It was no more than a dozen paces from back door to front. His green cardigan with the hole at the elbow lay draped over the settee. Here on the low walls and propped up between the shelves and the chests were portraits of men with fierce features and unruly hair leaping from dark canvases, Victorians no doubt from their costume, but unkempt and unaccommodated. These were men of strong opinions and stern disciplines whose portraits kept alive in this cottage a vision of themselves.

"Family but not family" Louis had said of these people, and named two or three with biblical names, not Matthew and Luke but still evangelical names, as if it were a little-known Dorsetshire gospel they had told. It was Louis's gift, which Maggie felt at every visit, that whatever was around him was made larger in his ambience, whether books or pictures or talk or even the tea and biscuits that he served from the pale green cups that lacked handles or the plates missing flakes of china. Walks with Louis that went no further than the nearby fields and woods traversed continents and centuries.

She left the cottage to walk up to the churchyard. It lay at the top of the hill, quietest spot in the quiet village. Louis's grave was in the far corner under the yews, marked by a stone cross bearing the legend: Louis Yeoman, born 9 March 1859, died 1 October 1916. He was only 57, she realised in surprise. He seemed much older ... but no, it wasn't older that he seemed but wiser. He was a mature man (the word came unbidden to her mind), mature like good wine or ripe fruit, and she wondered if this might be something very rare in human beings. She'd assumed that maturity was automatic, like ageing, but when she thought of the old men and women she knew, they tended rather to sourness or hardness, like apples better left to the wasps.

Louis was English through and through, she supposed. She'd never heard of roots that belonged further away than Devon. Yeoman, a good old English name, Louis said. Yeeman, he said it must have been originally, man of the land, of the earth, from the Greek. She had wondered how an old English name could come from the Greek, but he said that names had longer and more marvellous histories than kings and castles and assured her that it was so. He had a strange accent when he talked, peculiar to himself. An old Celtic accent perhaps, or Goidelic or Fomorian. He would pronounce Africa as Aafrika, with a long 'a' at the start. 'Aafrika,' she remembered him saying, 'a *civilised* country.' What was uncivilised to him was this new barbarism of the West, masquerading as progress, this multiplying greed raised to the status of a religion. It was as old as Mammon, he said, and according to him the so-called Great War was being fought between the servants of Mammon.

'Let them go and fight it out themselves,' he said, 'let the bankers put on uniforms and the empire builders man the frigates and the moneymongers take up arms. Let the violence stay with those who bred it, I say, and let the common folk get on with what they like to do. I tell you, Maggie, that they will not always stand for it. They will not always endure the deceits of the politicians and the bragging of the generals. There will come a time, Maggie, when the people will heave the whole top-heavy structure *into the sea*!'

When he became indignant, his voice swelled and rose, and the peculiar Fomorian accent grew spiky and threatening. Maggie Fox knew that in some incomprehensible way the war had killed him too, and silenced him. She sat by his grave recalling his emphatic voice and the frown he wore when he listened and the day she had visited and he was ill in bed, sitting up like an eagle-eyed old bird. She got up and picked sprigs of rosemary from a bush by the graveyard gate and strewed them on the earthen bump that contained all that was left of Louis Yeoman, to whom she felt she owed her life. But when the tears came to her eyes, they were not for Louis who was dead but for Jack who was still alive, and she angrily wiped them away and ordered them not to trouble her with their girlish sentiment. Jack would come to Hammond. Despite what the priest had said.

When she had come to on his infernal couch after her fall from the horse, she had wanted to search for Jack. That was her business, the priest had told her, and he would have none of it. She had stepped outside but only for a moment. The fog was as thick as ever and there was no sound, as if the whole world were gone away. Her shoulder ached from the fall and her head from the poisoned tea. Her eyesight was fragile, as if her view of things might again splinter and fragment, and the thought filled her with fear. When she went in, the priest spoke to her again but she had trouble in following his words. He told her which bedroom she could use and lit her a lamp. As she had climbed the stairs, he had come to the bottom of the staircase and called after her. 'In the morning we shall find him by the Giant,' he had said.

She had woken when it was still dark and crept downstairs with her lamp, planning to get away on foot before he was up. When she heard someone move in the stables, it had been the man he called his slave, who had looked at her shyly and had gestured to the yard. 'What is it?' she said and he had replied by bending his head forward and putting his index fingers pointing upward by the side of his head to make the sign of a horse.

'The horses are here?' she asked and he nodded, quietly opening the stable door for her and following her outside. The horses were on the verge beyond the yard and they moved away when she went to them, but they came at once to the silent man as if they had known him of old and he stroked the black filly and held her for Maggie to get up.

She thought he would leave her then but instead he took the filly by her halter and led them onto the causeway over the marsh, and all the way to the highway he led them, where she thanked him kindly and rode off, but never a word did he utter. His master, the priest creature, had not stirred. She was done with him, she thought.

She was not. As Maggie sat by Louis's grave, the priest creature was seated in Louis's armchair, reading in his journals. On his arrival in the room, his eye had run over the scholarly volumes, the bulky histories, the literary classics, and fixed on the bottom shelf, packed tight with monographs, excavation records and a series of blue-bound manuscripts which were the journals of Louis Yeoman. The first, dated 1878, was made up of continuous prose written in a hand looped and effortful, not yet adult. In the succeeding volumes, the writing became better marshalled and compact. The last of all, started in August 1914 and containing brief notes and sketches, was set down in a dense, minimal script. The last entry was for April 9, 1916: 'Herons nesting at Monks' Pool', followed by a poem of four words on four lines, which ran 'Dolmen, omen, ominous, moon', like the declension of a very irregular Latin noun. There were nine journals altogether, each in the same blue binding.

The priest made his way through the journals, starting with the most recent, glancing at first lines, headings, sketches, sentences underlined. He stopped at a short essay entitled 'Barrows and Witches', which he read without pause or expression:

We live in secular times. We pay less and less attention to ritual, and certainly to magic. Most of us have no clear idea of what magic is.

Conjuring tricks for children, weird gatherings to make contact with the dead, incantations with no more power than is given them by superstition. Magic has been put to flight by the so-called enlightenment, consigned to the darkness of the occult. Yet everywhere save in the 'enlightened' West, the magical world is indubitably alive, and to this magical world, obeying laws incomprehensible to science, certain human matters indubitably belong, among them the matter of death. Who would toss a dead body in a hedge? Only a desperate outlaw. Who would willingly sleep in the same room as a corpse of the recently dead? Not even this desperate outlaw.

But even in our de-magicked world, we are still blessed with some of the old perceptions. Just as a dog will choose to lie over a hidden spring, we still react to unseen influences. Occasionally – too occasionally, alas – we are subject to *illumination*. Forgotten divinatory powers awake in us momentarily, not long enough for us to divine their purpose perhaps, but long enough to become aware of the pulse of the immaterial world vibrating in the world of matter. In this moment, the physical laws are suspended. Ancient stones summon, old tracks glimmer faintly in the dusk. Springs of water enchant, the wind makes messages in the trees and the curlews cry from quite another world.

The round barrows lie on paths of psychic energy perceptible to alert and solitary walkers. The barrow builders knew what was known by those who set up the dolmens and the cromlechs and in turn it was known by the early Christians, whose church bells chime over the same ways where stand the tumps and the toots, the sacred groves, the holy springs and the great trees – the *marked* trees, singular trees with singular histories.

If these sacred ways are channels of energy, we may ask whether people found a way of harnessing it. Were burial sites and toots and standing stones sited in order to enhance the flow of energy or in order to utilise it? Well. Christian churches were in all likelihood situated on these lines in order to counter or exorcise whatever energy or power is in question. The power was seen by the Christian ministers as pagan and therefore dangerous. But for the bronze age burials, the purpose was quite different. The presence of the psychic energy was viewed as an aid to the journey after death. *It was an aid to journeying.* But how was it known to be so? From instinct or experience?

Travel in the so-called astral plane is a commonplace among the spiritualists and also, by reputation at least, among the witches and the wizards and among the djinns of the east. Broomsticks and night-mares. Flying carpets. I cannot envisage this travel as taking place on the plane perceived by the five senses ... no, I cannot seriously picture old Sarah or Betty mounting the broom and firing off through the open window ... so I must either treat this travelling as a metaphor for mental travel, or I must allow of the possibility of travel in a parallel world, one that can be appre-hended by the senses only under specific and extraordinary conditions. I believe that the witches, who are the survivors of the old traditions of sorcery and magic, are concerned precisely with these conditions. The cauldrons and brews and charms and costumes and runes and rituals are the outward forms for the cultivation of inner states. They are partly of symbolic value and partly to distract the inquisitive and the inquisitors.

The witch hunts of the past were the product of ignorance and fear and a loss of awareness of the spiritual dimension. We like to think of them as having happened elsewhere: in Yorkshire if we live in the southwest, in England if we live in Scotland, in Essex if we live in Sussex. The truth is that they were common to all parts of this island, even in this pleasant corner of England where I write.

In Cerne there was an annual rite called the 'Hunting of the Spirits' which took place at Halloween. There was a beating of kettle drums, weird costumes, a fife and a fiddle. The route taken by the hunters went by tumps and toots, by crossroads and church spires, by barrows long and round. The purpose of the procession was to scare off the spirits of the dead and root out those who had contact with them. Once the victim was a woman known as Peg who lived alone on the marsh with her herbs and roots and cats, and chickens that laid all year round. They took her and trussed her and bore her with them, over their shoulders. A mock trial took place, during which two unusual dice found in the woman's possession were held as evidence against her. At the trendle, by the Giant, a rough cage was fashioned of ash branches strung together. A bonfire was built, and in the cage the woman was burned.

Margery told me this story. She said that it was not the only time that one of her people had been burned alive. The Margarets keep these stories alive, lest they be forgotten. The dice may have been the very dice dug up by Austin Kelynack in the summer of 1878, or exact replicates. Our barrow was bronze age, with a medieval burial where the dice were found among ashes, charred bones and blackened teeth.

Maggie Fox saw the bright badges of colour on the rump of the pie-bald stallion from the top of the hill. The border collie sat by the side of its master's horse and growled at her as she passed. The back door was ajar and when she went in to the front room, the priest was in Louis's armchair, with the gun stood at his side.

'"22 January 1901",' he read, without looking up. '"Queen Victoria died. Does it matter?" The old man didn't care for royalty it seems.'

'How dare you read his journal?' Maggie Fox said. She held out her hand to take the notebook, but he ignored the gesture.

'How dare you come uninvited and unwanted into his house?'

There could be nothing private about books, the priest said. 'That's the whole point of them from the writer's point of view.'

'Listen,' he said, flicking through the pages of the journal till he came to the passage he wanted. '"The desire to put pen to paper is always a desire for immortality, and as long as the paper survives, the desire may be achieved, for even if one person should read the words, ten years or a hundred years' hence, the occasion they were written and the mind that hatched them is momentarily resurrected." You should be grateful to me for being the cause of a resurrection.' But still he never looked at her.

'I'm grateful to you for nothing,' she said. 'Please leave this house.'

'Two of the horses tethered outside are stolen,' he said. 'Regard me as a citizen doing his duty, tracking a deserter and a horse thief.'

'It is not your business, and anyway it is not why you are here.'

'Then why am I here, vixen?' he said.

'Not for a citizen's duty,' she said.

'I am here to take you to Jack Yeoman on the Giant,' said the priest.

'I shall wait for Jack here. On my own.'

'Then you will wait a long time,' he said. 'Jack Yeoman will be at the Giant. He told me so last night while you were … resting.'

'You poisoned me.'

'While you slept, I urged Jack Yeoman to hide out in a big city to save him from being apprehended by the army. However, he pays attention only to the dice, which pointed to the Giant. It would be advisable for us to join him as soon as possible. A man on a bare hill will not long escape the attention of the townspeople living below it.'

'Then I shall ride to the Giant. But there is no need for you to accompany me.'

'It would not be gentlemanly to allow a young woman to ride alone.'

'It is not gentlemanly to trespass on another person's property and to nose among his personal possessions. You are no gentleman. You are no priest.'

'I am a priest of ways of which you have no comprehension.'

'Then they are the ways of evil.'

The priest shrugged. 'Evil is a word used by the ignorant of things they fear,' he said.

'I have no fear of you,' she lied.

'Then accept my protection on your journey to the Giant.' He gestured towards his gun.

'Protection against what? The cows or the cowherds?'

'I can tell you for a certainty that your life is in danger.'

'Your attempts to scare me are ridiculous.'

'What is ridiculous is your childish notion that the world is as cosy as you have been taught. At every moment there are powers that threaten you. They are kept at bay by domestic routines and familiar illusions. Such things are now gone from your life. You are the mistress of a deserter in a dead man's empty house. You are aware of evil, because you used the word, but you do not know when and where it will raise its head. If I am the priest of evil, then you should be guided by me.'

'Give me Louis's notebook and get out,' she said. She grabbed the book from where it lay open on his lap, but he caught the other end of it and would not relinquish it to her. They stared at each other over the disputed book and in his eyes was an insolent gleam. Around them the silence pressed, the silence of the cottage and the village and the land. Being on her feet, the advantage lay with her. She gave a sharp tug on the journal and it slipped from his hand, but the sudden freedom made her lose her balance and she fell. He rose unhurriedly from the chair, picked up his gun and pointed it down at her.

'You and I have an appointment, long foretold,' he said.

Outside the dog barked. The priest turned his head to see through the window. Maggie pulled herself into a sitting position and when she looked up she saw Jack's face pressed against the glass. She saw the change in his expression as he took in the scene on the floor inside the room.

The handle of the front door rattled and was still again. With a contemptuous look at Maggie Fox as she sat on the floor, the priest covered the few feet to the front door.

'If not now, then later,' he said, turning to her. He unlocked the door and went.

Outside, John French scurried from the roadside and launched himself at Bill Bate who had appeared at the corner of the cottage. The man raised his arm and the dog went after it, springing with his whole body free of the ground. Bate took a step back, then as the dog landed at his feet, swooped down and caught the animal by the scruff of its neck. He whisked it from its feet and threw it in a bundle into the road.

The priest lifted the rifle to his shoulder, but Bate marched up and grabbed it by the muzzle, wrenching the gun from his hand. He tossed up the gun, caught it by the stock and in the same movement swung it downwards to deal the priest a terrible blow above his left eye. The priest went down, felled.

'Look out for that dog,' Jack called out, but whatever had been John French's intentions, he changed his mind when Bate turned to face him and slunk off to the other side of the road, where he stood watching, body low to the ground, ears cocked, dark eyes unmoving.

Jack crouched over the priest's body, looked at the pallid face and put his ear close to the man's lips.

'You killed him, Bate,' he said, looking up.

'I hardly touched him,' Bate said.

'Hardly touched him?' Jack pointed to the bloody gash by the priest's eyebrow. 'You dented his skull.'

'He's never dead,' Bate in a tone of puzzlement. 'I swung his little gun at him to teach him a lesson, no more'n that.'

'I know what a dead man looks like,' said Jack.

He went inside the cottage and found Maggie Fox crouching in the armchair pulling her jacket about her.

'Bate killed him,' Jack said.

She nodded.

'It's what he deserved,' Jack said.

She looked up at him sharply. 'Did he? Is that the price? Should that be the price?'

'He was threatening you with a gun. What did he want of you?'

'He wanted me to come to the Giant. He said that the dice told you to go there.'

Jack frowned. 'He was lying. He threw the cross, not the pillar.'

'Please let's leave,' Maggie said.

'To go where?'

'Anywhere but here. Return the horses. Find Charles. Go *home*.'

When Jack stepped outside, Bate stood by the porch puzzled and shrunken. He helped Jack shift the priest's body into the porch where they propped it into a corner. Jack took up the shotgun and handed it to Bate.

'Here,' he said. 'You'd better look after this.'

Bate took it and watched Jack go through the priest's pockets. He saw him draw something from the inside pocket, then clear the leaves from the lid of the water barrel and there cast two dice which tumbled briefly and were still. He could not guess at what strange game was being played over the body of the man he had murdered, but he learned what the dice read at least, because Jack called it like a piker at a fair.

'Circle Six!'

Maggie Fox heard it from inside the cottage and wished she had not. They covered the body with a blanket. When they rode off, they took the priest's piebald stallion with them, but Bate refused to ride it, marching at its side with the gun over his shoulder. All the road long he remained silent.

Chapter Seven

Last of the Six

Imagine the land like a board game seen from above. Not so difficult in this middle Dorset, where the hills are modest, the woodlands are copses, the rivers brooks, the valleys dingles, and the fields tillable by a man and a horse in a day. Think of the territory of the Margarets' dice as a circle which might be crossed by a man on foot in a couple of hours. Detach it from the busy markets and highways north and south. Remove the thudding of hooves and the turning of wheels, the chatter of people and the song of birds, the munching of cattle, the murmur of brooks, the rustle of leaves and the soughing of the wind, and look down on a silent kingdom made of imperceptibly changing patterns obeying the seasons and the weather and the dominions of man. (Louis Yeoman, *Journals*)

CHARLES YEOMAN kept the same round every evening – stables, cowstalls, piggery, rabbit hutches and hen coops, always in that order, starting with the largest and most precious animals and ending with the small and expendable. Even the chickens had their fences examined and the doors to their coops checked, and after them Charles would look in on the equipment and the tools, making sure that everything was in its place. One year after being wounded on the Marne, he walked with a slight limp and he still could not ride a horse in comfort, but he was not one to draw attention to infirmity, and even when alone, the limp was hardly discernible because the captain made sure that it was not.

When his mother had died, he was eighteen and he grew more solemn and more impatient of weakness. Two days after her death he had hidden in the apple store and wept until his lungs hurt and after that he wept no more.

That was ten years ago, and that same year his father began his gradual retirement to Hammond, leaving the Manston house and farm in the hands of his eldest son. His father had run the farm off-handedly, trusting things to take care of themselves, giving more time to his books than to his fields, a farmer in name but a scholar by choice. If the barn roof leaked, the answer was a handily placed bucket; if a harness broke, string would do the job until it broke once more. The bullocks trampled through the hedges and the chickens got among the vegetables.

When Charles took over, all this changed. The farm workers didn't always care for the changes, but the cattle grew fatter, the milk was more, and leaks in roofs were fixed the same day. Inexplicably, there were fewer maggots in the apples. He was his mother's son was the way Charles saw it, and the more years that passed since her death, the truer this seemed to be to him. In Charles's eyes, Jack was like his father, full of unnecessary ideals and pointless notions. Refusing an army commission was typical of him. What possible object was there in entering the ranks when an officer's training was offered? Why should one follow when one might lead? It had been the same at school, where Jack had turned down the chance of being a house prefect. Charles saw this not as a rejection of privilege but a denial of duty.

On the morning of the last day of October 1916, Charles was

surprised that Maggie Fox was not at breakfast. Always they break-fasted together at seven o'clock. When she failed to appear, he knocked on the door of her room. Getting no reply, he went in, thinking that she might be unwell. The bed had not been slept in. On the bedside table was the note in Jack's handwriting: '*I'll be in The Giant's Club at Cerne tonight and tomorrow night.*' Charles went at once to Jack's room and saw a drawer open. Under the bed he found the uniform, bundled up. He took the unsigned note down to the breakfast table with him and set it by the teapot. At intervals between scrambled eggs and buttered toast and several cups of tea, Charles pondered Jack's message. He called the housekeeper and told her he would be gone for the rest of the day and maybe longer. He dressed in his captain's uniform and packed a bag with a few things for a night's stay. He looked for his Spanish jacket and found it gone. When he went to take out the Zenith, that was gone as well. He found his head-man, Frank, in the milking parlour, gave him instructions for himself and the other men and told him to send his boy for the carter. While waiting he paced up and down, rehearsing what he would say to Jack. His brother's absence from the line (he would not call it desertion) deeply disturbed him, but the disappearance of the jacket and the motorbike made him angry. He was not good at waiting. When Frank didn't know when the coach left Sturminster for Cerne, he told him to go and find someone who did. The answer came back 'nine o'clock', which was what he had thought in the first place. When the carter picked him up, Charles told him that there was little future in being a carter with such an old horse and the carter told him to mind his own business. And so they proceeded slowly and without further talk down the road towards Sturminster. There he called at the post office and sent the following telegram to an acquaintance at the War Office in London: 'Very concerned about my brother L/Cpl Anthony Yeoman of the Sixth Light Infantry (C Coy. Sixth Battalion). No news two months. Enquire and inform most urgently. Reply here with copy to Post Office, Cerne Abbas, Dorset.' He took the coach at nine and was in Cerne by midday. His first call was to *The Giant's Club* where he spotted Maggie's bicycle leaning against the wall in the yard. In the inn he ordered a cup of coffee and had a talk with the landlord. This began with the weather and the crops and the cost of ale and how quiet things were keeping in wartime Cerne with half the men gone and half the horses too and hardly any livestock at the markets and no trade to speak of. "What, no visitors,' said the captain. 'Almost none,' the answer came back. 'No visitors last night?' The landlord was cautious at first, eyeing the captain's uniform, but the story soon came out about the young man who had spoken out against the war and how Bill Bate had warned him to keep his mouth shut and how there was a young woman there too, who must have been his girl.

'Nonsense,' said Charles. 'She's one of the family.' *His girl?* The idea was strange and irritating.

Then it should have been the captain's turn to say what he knew, but he had no time to waste for that, nor inclination either. Where had the pair gone after they left, he wanted to know, but the landlord couldn't say for sure. Charles finished his coffee and walked down the cobbled high street to the post office.

There a cable awaited him which ran: 'Very much regret Jack Yeoman listed missing in action. Keep hoping. Will investigate and inform. Sincerely, Maurice.' This news did not affect the captain's plan, but it bought him time. He returned to *The Giant's Club.*

'I need a horse and trap,' he said.

These days it might not be easy, the landlord told him. Where was the captain trying to get to if he might ask. Hammond, the captain said, whereupon the landlord clicked his tongue and shook his head.

'Ask around then,' said Charles, 'and meanwhile be good enough to bring me some lunch.' He positioned himself in the window overlooking the high street where the landlord brought him cold roast beef and cold roast potatoes and something he called military pickle which sounded to the captain suspiciously like a comment on the conduct of the war. The beef, however, was excellent.

During lunch, an unusual wagon with a hooped canvas cover drew up outside *The Giant's Club,* which Charles at first took to be a Romany caravan. The driver was a short, wiry, dark-skinned individual with black, curly hair, but there was something smart about his appearance. The shirt seemed too clean and the jaw too close-shaven for a gypsy. Besides, the man was on his way in and the gypsies rarely came inside public houses. When he asked for a beer, his accent was London not West Country and nor was his manner that of a traveller.

'Let me stand you that,' said the captain, drawing his purse from his pocket and stepping up towards the bar.

The wagoner looked at him quizzically. 'Why not, if that's your pleasure,' he said.

'It is,' said the captain, 'and it'll be my pleasure to lay two shillings alongside those two pennies if you'll be my driver for the afternoon.'

'I thank you for the drink, Captain, but that's all the business there'll be between us. I have got a fair way to cover today, and me services as a driver are not available.'

'Five shillings, then.'

'It's a tidy offer, but the answer's still no.'

'Which way are you headed?'

'Dorchester, for a start.'

'Dorchester's not far and it's only midday,' the captain said. 'You'd have time to take me where I want to go – a couple of hours there and back, say – and still get to Dorchester before nightfall.'

'It doesn't fit with my plans,' said the wagoner. 'If you'll allow me, I'll just wet my whistle here and continue on my way.'

'Half a sovereign,' Charles said.

The landlord, who was following the negotiation carefully, looked at the captain in surprise. The wagoner took a long sup of his ale.

'No more than an hour to get there, you say?'

'About that.'

'All right, then. When do we start?'

'As soon as you've finished your beer.'

Charles took a half-sovereign from his purse and put it on the bar to seal the transaction and the man eyed it before picking it up and thrusting it in his pocket.

'Come along then, Captain,' he said. 'The old lady takes her time on these roads and I won't be hurrying her, ten shillings or not.'

They set off at a leisurely pace northwards out of Cerne, along the same road Jack and Maggie had taken the day before. To Charles's questions, the wagoner gave perfunctory answers: Cockler was his name, London his native city and westwards lay his destination.

'What's your line of business?'

'My business is my own, I suppose,' said Cockler.

'Naturally. But there must be some reason for your journey. West-wards, you say, but what awaits you there?'

'The same as awaits any man who must work for his daily bread. A job, a roof over his head.'

'Why westwards then? Such things can be found anywhere.'

'Is that so, Captain, in your experience?'

'From my own experience, I cannot say so. I'm talking generally. Generally speaking there are jobs to be had everywhere, I believe.'

'Generally speaking doesn't help much, Captain. It's specifics what count, see. Specifically you might find it very difficult to pick up some paid employment where I come from, for example. Specifically I might find it well nigh impossible to get a job on a farm in these parts, unless I were known to someone. People don't like to take on strangers, that's the long and the short of it.'

'What about the army?' said the captain sharply. 'They're after any-one who can raise a rifle.'

'That's true, Captain, as none would know better than yourself. But I tried that, you see, and it was discovered that I had a condition.'

'A condition?'

'A condition that prevented me doing my military duty.'

'What sort of condition, may I ask?'

'You'll ask whether you may or not, Captain, aren't I right? No offence taken but,' said Cockler. 'A condition they couldn't rightly put a name to, but it's kept me from my duty as you see, and I don't mind telling you it's affected my search for other kinds of job as well.'

'They must have some idea of what's wrong with you.'

'It's a kind of nausea, you could say.'

'Problem with the innards, then.'

'A kind of nausea is the way I put it. Comes on without warning but what an awful mess when it does!'

'There's my damned motorbike,' Charles shouted suddenly, standing up and pointing indignantly towards the verge.

'Hold hard, Captain. Don't rock the boat. It's a bit steep right here so if you'll stick a rock behind the wheel then we can make a stop.'

Cockler reined in and the rig came to halt alongside the Zenith. Charles hopped down on to the road, wedged a rock under a wheel and strode over to his motorbike. He picked it up, tried the kickstart a few times and checked the fuel.

'Typical of him,' he said. 'Stole my bike and never even looked at the fuel. Now, Cockler, if you can give me a hand to load this up onto the back of your wagon, we may not have to go all the way to Hammond. We'll track down some petrol and then I can be on my way and you can be on yours.'

Cockler climbed slowly down from his perch, stood over the bike and shook his head.

'Great lump of machinery,' he said. 'I don't know that there'd be room for it. Better if we try at the next village for some fuel and then ride back with it.'

'Suppose there's no fuel at the next village, or the one after that? We'll be losing time. Just pitch some of your stuff further into the wagon, won't you, and then we'll haul her up. You from above and me from below.'

Cockler was unenthusiastic.

'Pitching my stuff here and there may seem all very well to you, Major,' he said, 'but how do you know it's the sort of stuff you can pitch? Generally speaking you may think that a bloke's stuff can be pitched at will, but on this specific occasion, I may not be so keen.'

'Very well,' said Charles curtly. 'It's your stuff of course.'

'That's so,' said Cockler. 'However, if you'll just hold your horses a bit, we can see what we can do.'

He climbed up into the back of the wagon and unhurriedly began seeing what could be done. Charles sat on the bank and watched impatiently.

'That should do the trick,' said Cockler, coming to the edge of the wagon.

'Now let's see about lifting the bike.'

'As I said,' said Charles. 'Me from below, you from above.'

The captain could barely get the bike off the ground. Cockler leant down, grabbed it with both hands and heaved. Charles lost his grip on the machine and it was Cockler's muscle alone that pulled it onto the bed of the wagon.

'Now, Major, did you get any oil on your battledress?'

'That was well managed, I must say,' Charles said. 'It's captain, not major.'

'There's no army here, Major, so I suppose I can promote you or demote you as I see fit. By the by, you didn't mention why it is that you're stuck here in Dorset instead of off shooting Jerries.'

'Invalided out,' Charles said.

'Invalided out was it? Sort of what happened to me because of my condition, then. Only sometimes it seems that I've been invalided out of the whole world, if you see what I mean.'

'No, I don't,' said the captain.

'No? Well, it takes a bit of explaining, I suppose. We'll lead the old lady up the rest of this hill, shall we, what with the extra weight and the slope?'

At the top of the hill they climbed back on to the seat and soon came into Minterne. The captain directed Cockler to head for the Manor House. The bailiff was found but there was no petrol to be had in Minterne, he said, and he didn't rightly know where there would be any between Dorchester and Sherborne. He strolled round to the back of the wagon, inspected the Zenith, scratched his jaw and came back to the riders.

'That's a motorcycle,' he said.

'Right first time,' said Charles.

'That's maybe the same motorcycle as was left last night on the road outside the village,' he said.

'Correct,' said Charles.

'In that case, I reckon you'd best have a word with Mr Lawrence,' said the bailiff.

Charles was not especially eager to have a word with Mr Lawrence.

'Time presses,' he said. 'Perhaps I might see Mr Lawrence on my way back.'

'I don't think that would serve. I believe that Mr Lawrence would want to see you as soon as possible.'

The Manor House did not impose in the Georgian or Victorian style; it was built with an older and subtler sense of proportion. The doorways were modest, the ceilings not unnaturally high, the light from the windows soft and oblique. The captain asked the butler to show him where he could wash his hands before he saw the squire, and this gave him the chance to straighten his uniform, comb his hair and get rid of the dust of the road. In front of the washroom mirror, he stood to his full height and thrust out his jaw.

Mr Lawrence was seated at his desk in the study and did not get up as Charles entered the room.

'Please be seated Captain Yeoman,' he said. 'I am right in thinking that you are Captain Yeoman, am I not?'

Charles bowed slightly. 'I prefer to stand if you don't mind, sir,' he said. 'I am pressed for time. I wonder how you are aware of my identity, since I did not send in my name nor mention it to your bailiff.'

'By all means remain standing, Captain. This need not take long. Last night, your brother made off with two of my horses. He is, I am told, a deserter from the front. In my position as Justice of the Peace, both these matters concern me, as you may imagine, but the second is the more serious.'

'I was unaware of the first matter, sir, but no doubt there is an explanation. As for the second, I think you may safely leave it with me, as a ranking officer in His Majesty's armed forces.'

'An explanation for breaking into a man's stables and stealing two horses, the one of them, I may say, a valuable animal? Frankly, I doubt it.'

'I repeat: I was unaware of it. It appears that my brother is in a state of some confusion. Such things, as you know, are not unusual in the trenches. He is now on leave and in need of rest. I'm anxious to find him as soon as possible. Unfortunately my vehicle – the motorbike in question – requires fuel, and it is this that brought me to Minterne Manor.'

'My bailiff tells me that there is no fuel on the estate,' said Lawrence. 'Under the circumstances, I am not prepared to lend you a horse. The police have been informed of your brother's crime, Captain, and I prefer to leave the matter in their hands.'

'I don't think you quite see my point ... '

'It is you who do not see the point, Captain, and I can hardly expect that you would, with such a close personal involvement in this affair. Perhaps you are not aware that your brother last night preached treason in a local inn. He is on leave, you say, and I can hardly doubt your word as an officer, but no one has leave to make public statements against the war, and this falls within my jurisdiction not your own.'

Charles Yeoman was outranked but he was not outgunned. 'It is clear, Mr Lawrence, that you have no experience of trench warfare and its effects,' he said. 'You will find, sir, that this is an army matter and it is I who represent the army here. You are mistaken in thinking that I will be influenced by my personal feelings. Your horses will be returned by the morning. If you decide to press charges, that is up to you. I suspect that I will apprehend my brother long before the police get close to him. This is all I have to say.'

The captain bowed a second time, more stiffly than before, and left the room.

The bailiff had a further thought on the question of fuel. There was a miller in the village of Duntish who kept a motor car and sold petrol in the neighbourhood.

'It's more or less on the way to Hammond, Cockler,' Charles said, climbing up.

'I hope your coat keeps the rain out, Major,' said Cockler, gesturing at the sky. Black-bottomed clouds lined the western horizon, like a squadron of dark-hulled craft.

Chapter Eight

The Duntish Rings

The habit of celebrating Hallowe'en by lighting bonfires on the hills is not yet extinct and men still living can remember how people would wait until the last spark was out and then would suddenly take to their heels, shouting at the top of their voices, 'The cropped black sow seize the hindmost!' ... In Scotland, the boys went from house to house and begged a peat from each householder, usually with the words: 'Gie's a peat t'burn the witches.' (James Frazer)

BY Duntish Common under Dungeon Hill was an inn by the name of *The Duntish Rings*. The Rings were ancient banks or ramparts now hardly more than ripples in the grassland, long buried under bramble and scrub. The oldest part of the inn dated back two hundred and fifty years, with blackened oak beams you couldn't put a nail in and bottle-glass window lights and hardly a straight line in the walls or roofs or eaves. It had been built by a band of Blackfriars, but the band dwindled swiftly until there was only one, a tall, silent man who tried to make a garden out of the thin soil of that corner of the common but could raise nothing but broad beans and spinach, and whose fruit trees grew spindly, with fruit that was bitter and hard. And such may have been the character of his life under Dungeon Hill, whose great bulk reared over the house and kept out the sun for half the day, even in spring. When he died, the house was abandoned and none knew to whom the land belonged. Perhaps to the order of the friars, they thought, so they left it alone while the roof rotted and the

117

garden was taken over by nettles that grew head-high in summer, and badgers made their home in the cellar. Several times in two centuries newcomers came to squat or settle, for the friars' title was eventually dead and buried. The nettles were cleared and the roof was fixed. A porch or a shed or a barn was added, each in its own style and according to the new occupant's competence, so that by the end a stranger would be hard put to know which door to use to get to which part of the house. Only the garden remained the same: weedy plants and thin trees surrounded by a badly-built wall that someone had put up, bulging where it ought not and crumbling where it could.

Towards the end of the Victorian century came a man called Dooley and his wife, who were supposed Irish on account of their name, although their speech was West Country speech and they hailed only from Somerset, or so the man said. Dooley's idea was to set up an inn, and for a year or so he worked hard enough with hammer and trowel and paintbrush, and at the end of that time the inn sign was raised announcing the existence of *The Duntish Rings*. Dooley said that the name was his wife's idea, which didn't surprise anybody for his wife was known as a singular sort of person. She it was who painted the inn sign and it was reckoned rather fine, her rendering of grass ramparts with golden rings aloft, but even the prettiest sign, they said, wouldn't make much trade in that dull spot, which indeed proved to be the case. Nor did it surprise the people of Duntish when Dooley upsticked and left, without a word to his neighbours, leaving his wife in sole command of the inn, the house, the garden and the cats. Mrs Dooley was seen one morning with a paintbrush adjusting the wording on the signboard from *Thomas Dooley, Innkeeper* to *M. Dooley, Innkeeper*.

You could tell that she was a clever woman, they said, but that didn't mean she was easy to live with. Mrs Dooley continued to run *The Duntish Rings*, and they had to admit that she made a good fist of it; the taproom was always clean, the beer was never stale, and doors and windows were freshly painted. Even the garden showed some signs of being revitalised, with healthy-looking carrots and potatoes and parsnips coming up, and rows of beans that were better than those at Wootton Farm. Anyone with a scrap of land could grow such stuff as these, of course, but the wonder was that no one had before managed to do so on the corner of Duntish common under the hill. There still wasn't much trade, although some of the farm workers from Pulham and Wootton had taken to spending their spare coppers there of an evening. These working men, earning ten or twelve shillings a week and paying three or four of these in rent and leaving half-a-dozen with the wife to take care of, could rarely afford more than a penny a night for half-a-pint, so that there was more talking than drinking in the taproom of *The Duntish Rings* – and there was no charge for talk, was there? The regular drinkers had no complaints about the landlady, who they said was a decent sort of woman, intolerant of any blasphemous talk or smutty songs, but civil enough to those who were civil to her. Observant locals took note that there were sometimes bedrooms lit in the evenings, with their curtains drawn at night, suggesting that certain travellers were choosing to put up there. Some said there were other visitors during the day, who came and went by the door in the garden wall which gave directly on to the fields. It was assumed the travellers and visitors were of the poorer class, since there were neither carriages seen in the yard nor servants in the taproom. After the war broke out, overnight visitors were few. In the villages, young men were scarce and money was short. The taproom of the *Rings* often stayed empty.

On 31 October 1916, the weather turned wet in mid-afternoon and nasty by early evening. The worst of it seemed to gather around Dungeon Hill as if attracted by its dark mass and nautical shape, like a storm drawn to a ship at sea. On nights such as these, the big taproom at *The Duntish Rings* felt very much like the saloon of an ocean-going ship, with windows you couldn't see out of and no lights visible but its own. Upstairs, where none but Mrs Dooley and her overnight lodgers ever went, the wind came whistling round the side of the hill beating down from its flat summit and shrieking through the clumps of tall beeches on its flanks, and you would have thought that land was far off indeed, perhaps never to be seen again. Such a night was Halloween in the year that will always be known in this island as the year of the Somme. Mrs Dooley was on her own at *The Duntish Rings*. The girl who acted as scullion and chambermaid and assistant cook had the afternoon off to go and see her family and wouldn't be back until the next day, it being a three-hour walk to get there. Mrs Dooley well knew that the girl liked to be at her parents' house for the eve of All Hallows, although whether this was because on that spirit-filled night of the year she wanted to be close to her family or because she liked to be away from the ramshackle solitude of the inn, Mrs Dooley had no way of knowing. Despite the weather, Mrs Dooley did not expect to spend the evening alone. There had been signs. The cats were restless in the afternoon and when she had gone to feed the chickens, there was a brown rat stood on the feed bin looking at her. She threw her shoe at it and it only hopped up the haystack onto the wall-plate where it crouched under the slope of the roof and continued to look at her. 'Shog off, brown rat,' she said, but it did not. There were never rats in her barn. It was the cats' job to see to that, but the cats that day were patrolling the house. This alone alerted their owner to the imminence of the exceptional.

Mrs Dooley fed the chickens, returned to the house and built up the big fire in the taproom. She checked how much stew there was in the stewpot and how many logs in the log-pile. Not many things could make Mrs Dooley nervous, and being on her own wasn't one of them, but she liked a big fire on a wet night and she didn't enjoy scrambling in the woodshed for logs after dark.

The taproom was long and narrow, running from end to end of the front part of the house. Two large bow windows gave onto the yard with the outside door between them. The short north wall was occupied by an ingleside fireplace of generous proportions, with bays for the woodstacks at either side. A line of wooden pews stood in a rough semi-circle round the fireplace. Along the inner wall of the room were low trestles holding six barrels, two for the best bitter, three for the ordinary and one that stayed empty. The ordinary went faster, priced at a farthing a pint less. At the southern end of the room was a large round refectory table not much used in winter being too far from the fire. Beyond this table was the door leading to the scullery.

When she'd lit the lamps, Mrs Dooley made herself comfortable in her seat in the corner of the ingleside, a tall straight-backed armchair, upholstered in dark red chintz, with a stool to match. Mrs Dooley took little account of foul weather, but saw no reason to be cold in her own home, and she would bake there pleasantly of an evening, keeping her hands busy with the shelling of nuts if it were the season or stoning the plums for the jam and her ears busy with the talk from the pews. Regular drinkers at *The Duntish Rings* had been heard to speak of the landlady's seat as her throne, referring not so much to the grandeur of the chair as to the royal ease of its occupant.

About five o'clock, Mrs Dooley heard horses splashing through the puddles of the yard. Soon after, a young man, dark and wet, put his head round the door and she spoke to him from her fireside seat, telling him to put the horses in the barn and to take hay from the stack and grain from the bin.

'You'll have to make shift for yourselves,' she said.

'That'll be no trouble to us, Missus,' said the young man. 'Come on in, Maggie,' he called out over his shoulder and his head disappeared.

A moment later a girl came swiftly and quietly through the door and scanned the room. Mrs Dooley watched as she approached the fire. This Maggie was no more than nineteen or twenty, but what self-possession, wet though she was. She came right up to the fire and said good-evening in a bell-clear voice before taking off her dripping jacket and coming up close to the flames.

'It's wretched weather,' she said.

''Tis not the weather that's wretched, but the wretches that must be out and about in it,' said Mrs Dooley. She went to fetch a clean towel from the scullery and wondered why a well-spoken young girl should be travelling on horseback in such weather and what was the source of the trouble that hung about her, but when the young man returned she knew at once part of the answer, because when the girl looked up to see the man there was a look on her face that could not be mistaken.

'We got caught in the storm,' the man said.

'If you want a hot drink there's tea or there's rum and hot water,' the landlady said.

They chose rum and she brought it in two green-glass tumblers, adding steaming water from a kettle that stood on a stone close to the flames. The two of them stood by the fire with the drink cupped in their hands. The man's face told of boldness. Born under a fire sign, probably. Perhaps the Lion. The girl had lovely eyes, clear and strong like her voice, and there was that stillness in her, despite her anxiety. Her sign was air, surely, the Scales or the Water Carrier. Fire feeds on air, but air does not burn. Yet Mrs Dooley had never seen two people so close in spirit divided by so wide a gulf.

The girl didn't look at him but she registered his slightest movement. Manlike, he seemed oblivious of her. She loved him and he didn't love her in return? Something more complex than this. Was he ill? He looked strong enough, his colour was good. But he was restless and distracted, and once when Mrs Dooley saw him staring into the flames, she divined in him a despair so immense that it hit her like a wave.

A second, older man came in.

'Name's William Bate from Cerne,' he said nodding to her.

Here was a different soul. A big, simple soul of a kind common enough in these Dorset vales. Yet this big fellow was troubled too.

'Will you take a drink, William Bate from Cerne?' she said.

'Willingly, Missus, if I had the means to pay for it,' said Bill Bate. 'We came unexpected, to get out of the rain, and I wasn't prepared for expenses.'

'You paid for my drink, Bate, and now I'll pay for yours,' said the young man.

'Fair enough, Jack Yeoman,' said Bate.

So Mrs Dooley learned the young man's name, and learned, too, that there was no very long acquaintance between these two, that Bate was neither servant nor workman to the other, which made her wonder why they travelled together.

'We'll have our drink, then, and look at the weather, and carry on to Minterne,' said Bate.

'I don't think so,' said Jack Yeoman. He felt for something in his pockets before glancing in the landlady's direction and seeming to change his mind.

'Depends on the storm,' he said.

'I'll want to get back tonight,' said Bill Bate.

But the rain was coming down in a steady downpour, it was almost dark and thunder sounded not far off.

'When did you eat, Jack?' the girl said, and he replied that apart from a chicken leg for breakfast and a few apples around midday he hadn't eaten, so she suggested taking a meal while they could.

'Is there anything in the pot, landlady?' he asked.

'I don't keep an empty pot hanging over the fire, Mister,' she said. 'But I'll put in a handful of fresh vegetables if you want to eat.'

Please do, he said, and so it was that Mrs Dooley was in the scullery peeling carrots and chopping up onions when the next visitor arrived. She heard voices and an exclamation and when she returned to the taproom with the pan of vegetables, there was another man there in a captain's uniform. She saw at once that he was family. He was shorter

125

and older and neither as dark nor as handsome as the first, but you couldn't miss the resemblance. He was brother, or cousin at least, and he behaved familiarly with the girl, as with a younger sister. Mrs Dooley wondered whether Jack Yeoman might be married or engaged to the girl, but the girl wore no ring and on balance she thought not. Mrs Dooley tipped the vegetables into the stew, lowered the pot on its pot-hook and built up the fire.

The door opened and there entered a man with the light step of a dancer and lines of laughter around his bright eyes. He shook his head and shoulders like a dog after a swim and stamped his feet on the doormat as if announcing his arrival to the room at large.

'Well knock me down!' he said, looking around. 'The Yeoman brothers meet. Good evening to you, ladies and gents.'

'How the devil do you know my brother, Cockler?' the one in uniform wanted to know.

'Same as I know yerself, Captain. Needing wheels on the Dorset lanes.'

Cockler turned to Jack. 'What's up, John?' he said. 'Sorry to bring yer brother to the party. I was bought for ten sovereigns like the feller in the bible.'

'Thirty pieces of silver,' Jack said.

'But that was weeping Jesus, and this is only Johnny Yeoman, former lance-corporal. How was I to know you was holed up in here? I thought we was hopping in for a hunk and a dram, which I was looking forward to. And still am.'

Mrs Dooley served another round of rum.

'No call for the water, thank you, Landlady,' Cockler said. 'We've

126

had it running down inside our collars for an hour and there's no need for it to spoil the grog as well.'

The captain took his rum with water. His was a shallower face than his brother's, Mrs Dooley saw, but not a weaker one. Decisive but unimaginative. Aries, she thought.

'We were making for father's cottage at Hammond,' said the captain. 'We heard that a man had petrol here in Duntish. The miller's got a Morgan three-wheeler. Motorcycle with a metal box built round it. Odd contraption. He sold us petrol but didn't ask us in out of the rain because we were so wet. If we hadn't been wet we wouldn't have wanted to come in, would we? He told us of this place and we came on here.'

He spoke only to the girl, avoiding looking at his brother, and Mrs Dooley understood that this was close to what troubled them all, this matter between the two brothers. One of the landlady's cats – it was Toddy – strolled in from the corridor, eased under tables, brushed past the legs of chairs and leapt noiselessly into the nook by the fire, where she made herself comfortable on the top of the log pile and surveyed the company between half-closed eyes. Mrs Dooley wondered what the cat saw and felt about these people. Toddy could spot a chicken bone fall to the floor even with her eyes nearly shut and looking the other way. Yet cats were not only concerned with the visible world. The aura of each of these people, in Mrs Dooley's opinion, was clearer to the cat that it was to her. To the cat, she thought, an aura was as obvious as the shape of a brow or the look in an eye, it was the peculiar light within which each person moved.

'We'll have a talk, shall we Jack?' said the captain. 'Show us to another room, Landlady, if you would, so we can be on our own for a few minutes.'

'This is the only one with a fire burning and lamps lit,' the landlady said. 'You can sit at the oak table and nobody will disturb you.'

She pointed to the round table at the far end of the room and fetched a lamp and wiped the dust off the surface of the table. This piece of furniture was as old as the room it stood in, being too large to go through the doors and almost too heavy to lift. With three or four men sat down to eat, the table weighed more than the diners. The black brothers had eaten here without talking, for such was their rule, and now the Yeoman brothers were to talk here without eating. It was an auspicious place for either of these activities, having attracted to itself an intangible presence, familiar enough to Mrs Dooley's cats, who treated the table with circumspection. Mrs Dooley also favoured this table, aware of its subtle influence. She polished it herself, a task more meditative than laborious.

The two brothers brought their drinks and sat down opposite each other. The captain sat at the far side of the table, facing the fire and the company, and did most of the talking. He kept his voice low, but both brothers had voices better at booming than hushing and anybody in the room with a mind to do so could follow what was said between them.

'Top up the rum, Jack old fellow?'

'No.'

'Right you are. I'll say what I've got to say straight out without beating about the bush. You're here in Dorset when you should by rights be with your regiment in France.'

'Rights? What rights?'

'Hear me out. Your reasons for being here are your own and we don't need to discuss them. You will have heard from Margaret of father's death. That would be reason enough for a visit home, lord knows.'

'God rest his soul.'

'However, the army will not see it that way … '

'No, they will not.'

' … unless you do exactly as I say, without question. You will return at once to France. I hoped you might be in Dover tomorrow morning, but tomorrow evening will have to do. I will issue you with a paper. It may not be quite what the regulations demand but it may serve, and in any case you will be returning urgently to your regiment and no one will stand in the way of that. I shall tell you what you will say to your commanding officer when you get there. You are listed as missing in action. I am sure that he will greet your reappearance only with relief. The weather may keep us here tonight. Tomorrow morning first thing you will come with me on the Zenith. We will pick up your uniform at Manston and you will be on the coach for Dover by mid-morning. Winchester, Southampton I expect, and along the coast.'

'Would that be by Battle or by Sandwich?'

'There is also the matter of Lawrence's horses. I cannot imagine what you were thinking of, helping yourself from his stables. However, let that be. If the horses are returned and you are on your way back to France, he may be persuaded to overlook the whole thing. The man who is with you, the big chap, who is he?'

'His name's Bate. One of the squire's men.'

'He can take the horses back then. Lawrence has already sent word to the police and this is why we have to make haste. Can I take it that you agree?'

'To what?'

'To all of what I have been saying.'

'Have the horses returned if you wish.'

'It's your going back to France I'm thinking of.'

'On that I cannot agree.'

'There is no alternative.'

Jack raised his eyebrows. 'No alternative? Of course there is. I can hand myself over to the army in Dorchester and declare myself a deserter.'

'Think of the consequences.'

'You've had your say, Charles. Now it's my turn. I can give myself up. Or I can disappear in a big city or in the remote countryside and hide out until the war's over. Or I can go to the anti-war groups – to Bertrand Russell and Lytton Strachey and the rest – and tell them what I've seen and what I know.'

'These men are cowards, and most of them are in prison where they belong. Besides, what you have seen and what you know is nothing more than what thousands have seen and know. Myself among them.'

'Each of us sees what we want to see. You see men brave enough to stand up against everything that people are saying around them and you call that cowardice. You see poverty and you call it obedience, you see death and you call it duty.'

'We have our differences. We always have had. You talk like your father. He always took your side.'

'Now we come to it,' Jack said weightily. 'If I was Louis's favourite son, why did he sign the farm over to you? Why didn't he give me half the land, or the buildings and fields at Lower Farm?'

'There was no need for that. He knew I'd look after you. What's more to the point is why did he go off to live by himself in a hovel? In the year you've been away, do you know how many times he called to see us? Once. It was because of me, whom he couldn't bear to see.'

'Charles, you're a fool. Don't you understand, it was because of mother? He didn't want to be in that house when she was not there.'

'That wasn't it.'

'Of course it was. I knew it, Maggie knew it, even Frank knew it. You couldn't see it because you never see beyond yourself.'

'Don't see beyond myself? Do you think it's myself I'm thinking about now?'

'In a way, it is. You think of the disgrace to the family if I'm caught. The blot against your name because of your brother.'

'*Vivere con honore o morire con gloria.*'

'To live honourably is to live by what you believe and not by what other people think.'

'You can't have honour by cutting yourself off from other people. Can an Indian fakir who spends his life staring at his navel have honour? No. Honour is about public recognition. Honour is bigger than self. Honour means doing what you must, even at the expense of your comfort or pleasure or fine ideals. Honour is duty. It's your duty to the memory of your mother and father, your duty to me and to Margaret, your duty to your country and to your fellow soldiers, to return to your regiment.'

131

'And I say it's my duty to the sanity of the human race not to go.'

'They'll shoot you then. They'll put you up against a wall and pin a piece of card to your breast and they'll shoot you as a coward.'

'But you'll know that they were wrong, Charles, won't you?'

'Will I?'

The voices of the brothers had grown louder. By the fire, Bill Bate was still on his feet, with a frown of deep deliberation. Now he set down his glass and crossed the room to where the brothers were seated.

'I overheard without wanting to,' he said to the captain. 'Your brother's no coward. I fought with him earlier on, see, and that's how I know it. There isn't a man in Cerne would willingly take me on with his fists, and I'm not boasting when I say so. Your brother needed for me to sit on him near enough before he'd give it up, and he caught me a couple of stingers that I can still feel now. I could see by the way he came at me that there was no yellow streak in him, and you ought to know that before you call him coward.'

'I didn't mean Jack was a coward. I meant only that he would be seen as such.'

'This afternoon,' said Bill Bate slowly, 'I killed a man.' He looked at each of them in turn, as if to make sure that everybody had heard him. 'He was a man I'd never met. The first minute I set eyes on him, I did away with him. He went down like a scarecrow and didn't get up. But when we picked him up to put him in the porch, he was heavy like a pig's carcass. As if what had gone out of him made him weigh more. Then I got to wondering whether this man I killed had sons or daughters, a wife, someone who loved him. Whether or not, he was still a

132

man. Now he's a sack of stuff that doesn't work. A damp sack in a porch.'

'What is this about, Jack?' said Charles.

'It was an accident,' Jack said.

'I went after your brother,' Bate went on, 'because he had deserted from the line and it made me angry thinking on it. Then I saw he was no coward and it should have made me wonder if there was another reason for not fighting. Now I've discovered it.'

'Who is this man you killed?' the captain asked.

'He was nobody, Charles. A meddler, a lunatic,' Jack said.

'He was a priest,' Bate said. 'If I'd seen the collar, I'd never have hit him.'

'He was no priest, at least,' said Maggie sharply.

'And where exactly is the body?' the captain wanted to know.

'Exactly in our father's porch,' said Jack.

'Why, for God's sake? Couldn't you have moved it somewhere, decently?'

'There is no decency in death, Charles.'

'Hammond is not the trenches. My father's cottage is not a mortuary. When someone dies, there are procedures to observe. These save us from savagery. You and I will go by Hammond in the morning and see to the corpse. We shall leave at first light. As for you, Bate, you can return the two horses to Minterne. Report the man's death to the squire.'

'Is everything now arranged to your satisfaction, Captain Yeoman?' Jack asked.

His brother looked at him darkly but made no reply.

'Accident or not, the man died and it was my hand that killed him,' said Bill Bate. 'I'll pay the price of his death, which is how it should be. But I've been thinking about this, because of what's going on over there.' He gestured beyond the house, beyond the darkening fields and forests, beyond the black waves, to where even at that moment armies of men were waiting on death. The three men who listened saw at once where Bate's gesture pointed and knew better than he did himself what was there. 'In the newspapers you get the feeling that what matters is how many for how many,' Bate said. 'Hundreds of theirs died but only a few dozen of ours. Like this was a good tally. That man died in Hammond and I'm still alive in Duntish. So that's all right then. I'm the winner. But death is the only winner, I'm thinking, and what puzzles me is how I never saw it before. It took killing someone to set me right.'

'It's the law that judges, Bate,' Charles said. 'If it was an accident, the law takes account of that.'

'You missed my point, Captain. It doesn't make it better or worse if they decide to string me up. It's two separate things. A life can't be paid for, not by another life and not by a thousand. The puzzle to me is this: if a man murders another man, he goes to hell for it. But if he pays for his crime here on earth, by hanging by the neck until he's dead, does he go to heaven after all?'

'At the front, heaven was when they ordered you back out of the way and the sun came out and dried your socks,' Jack said. 'Hell was when it was raining and you could hear the rats nibbling something at night and the shells began coming in. I thought more on the skinny ferryman than St Peter. The underground river and the ferryman

134

taking the last pennies from your pocket to punt you over to the land of the nameless dead – it seemed much closer. In the funk holes you could feel that river deep underneath, or something like it. He must have become a very rich man, the ferryman, when you come to think of it. Two obols a shot since the beginning of things. Tens of thousands of obols on July the first alone.'

'It's a wonder he ain't retired to a palace with fruit and wenches,' Cockler said. 'Trouble is, what wench would go near a bloke who'd been ferrying dead bodies for a living?'

'This talk is unhealthy,' said Charles. 'In the circumstances.'

'You're right as usual, Major,' Cockler said. 'It's why they gave you the pips. Not right for the ranks to talk of death. Unhealthy, as you say. Better for them to settle down to a nice game of cards and a cup of tea.'

'I have a game right here in my pocket,' said Jack Yeoman. 'Draw near to the table, friends and fellow travellers, and I'll show you how it goes.'

'What the devil is this?' Charles said.

'A game of dice,' said Jack. 'Bring your drinks and take a seat. The last supper's coming up, but first the dice must be cast.'

He reached into his pocket and drew out the red and white dice.

'I'll have none of this tomfoolery,' Charles said.

'Dying man's last wish, brother. We ask the dice a question and they give us the answer. Reading the options, you can call it. Six faces on the red die, six on the white. Thirty-six options in all, but the white die has only numbers so it's the red die that signifies. My question is this: what should a man do who has run away from a battle that he saw

135

nobody could win? No. What should a man do who refuses to fight for his country right or wrong even though thousands of his countrymen will go on dying?'

He held the red die up between thumb and forefinger, turning it as he spoke. 'Tower is prison or punishment. I give myself up to the army. Next, the circle. I've always thought of this one as meaning home, or the nearest thing to it. Right now I'm not sure where home is. I threw this today and it brought us here, to the round table. So let the circle mean: stay right here. Then sword. This is the fight, of course, but not the Somme, which is only madness. The sword means standing up for what I believe. Taking sides with the objectors and the pacifists and speaking out. After that, the pillar. It's the markstone, the guide on the road. To London or Penzance or the Highlands. And here's the skull. We've already covered the firing squad, so we'll take this to mean going back to the front. My brother's option. And lastly the cross. Tonight it signifies Christ's way. Turning the other cheek. I hardly know to whom I should turn it. Well, it's enough. Tower is arrest, circle is Duntish, sword is conscience, pillar is the road, the cross is Christ knows what and the skull is Charles. Forgive the shorthand, dear brother.'

He threw. The dice chased each other over the Blackfriars' dining table.

'Pillar One,' he read out. 'It's the road!'

There was a moment of silence, broken by Cockler, who stepped up to the table. 'May be so, John,' he said picking up the dice, 'but you've a damned funny way of arriving at it. To my way of thinking, a good choice is the one a man makes for 'imself, without the assistance of a pair of tricky fellers like these. Problem is with these little blight-ers that they come up with a different answer every time you ask 'em.'

He threw the dice. 'See here. Same question, John. But different answer, look. Ring Two. You get your girl.' He swept them up and threw again. 'Same question, mind. What next for Johnny Yeoman? Now what've we got 'ere? Five pillars. Skittles is it? A game of skit-tles? Landlady, do we have a skittle alley in the establishment? No? Wrong throw, let's try again.' A third time, he threw. 'Oh ho!' he said. 'Skull Six. Cockler, you've bleedin' well torn it this time. Six stiffs. We're all going to die! None of us is immortal! And there I was hop-ing that I'd slip the noose after all. You know how it is, John. We'll all be pushing up the daisies in the end, but somehow you go thinking that you might get away with it for another year or so. Then old age comes along, but still you're thinking, there'll be another month, or a week maybe, and by the end you're counting in days, but still you never guess the old gaffer with the sickle is going to catch up with you. He'll always be a step behind. But no. It's Skull Six, Johnny me lad. It's the philosopher's throw.'

'My father gave me these,' Jack Yeoman said, picking up the dice and examining them. 'His last gift before he died. I put them away and forgot about them. It was the evening before the first big attack that I got them out. In that dismal place without women or children or clean socks or an egg for breakfast. I thought they might say Skull One. Anybody might think so in that hole with the guns rumbling in the dark and the tin helmets hung up in a line. The odds were thirty-six to one against. I told myself even if it says Skull Two or Skull Three, it could be for other people. And it was six to one against getting the

137

skull at all. I thought of my father. You didn't know my father, Cockler. He was a … he was a serious man. I nearly said he was a deep man. Makes him sound like a well. That's not wrong actually. If you   lowered your bucket, it always came up with water. The currency of the dice was fate, not chance, he said. Those were his very words. So if I threw the dice or not, it wouldn't make any difference to what turned out. That was all decided long before. Then I threw.'

They were all watching him, thinking of the dismal hole and the rumble of guns and the helmets waiting for the heads.

'It was Skull Six. Not much philosophy needed to read that. The next day we went over the top. I don't know what the story was. The bombardment had gone off in the wrong place or the enemy had shifted their positions overnight. I ran on with the rest of them and nothing hit me. I was expecting it all the time, and around me people were going down. We couldn't find the break in the wire they'd told us would be there. We'd run the wrong way maybe. Run straight, they said, but we ran crooked. There was mud thrown up and smoke and yelling, and two or three of us came up against the wire and it might just as well have been a wall. You'd have ripped yourself to bits trying to crawl through it. Later the corporal came up with wire cutters. They'd shown us this bit in training. Snip here, snip there and it all comes apart. But it doesn't. It was like attacking a haystack with a kitchen fork and we'd been spotted by then so every time one of us stuck our heads up to try and get at the wire, the bullets came cracking through. We never got further than that. It was a small slope with the wire at the top and we lay there for hours. I can still see the bit of ground that lay right in front of my eyes. There was a clod of earth raised up with a tiny hollow underneath. No bigger than the hollow of your hand. But during the day, that clod grew to be a great rock and the hollow under it became the mouth of a cave. I imagined creatures living there,   minuscule human beings, dogs the size of crumbs, a troglodyte world. An ant came up out of the dark and for a moment it was a huge monster, until I got it back to scale again. I liked that ant. Got its home under a clod in no-man's-land. Plenty of stuff to feed on not far away. I thought if I crush it under my thumb it would be a crime. And that's the kind of soldier I became.

'Skull Six. Should have been skull sixty. They called us back in the end, and we weaved our way among bodies. I recognised one of them. Tom Cuff was his name. Quiet chap, pale face, with hair that stood up like a brush. Only time I talked to him, he told me about his two boys, one year old and three. His wife was very young, he said. They'd known each other since they were kids. He worried about her getting on without him.

'I never knowingly shot a man in six months. I fired away like the rest, but I aimed high or wide. All the time I knew I might have to kill one day, and that frightened me more than my own death. Once I wept, but it wasn't because I was afraid but because I was so *dirty*. I wondered how many of the others were doing what I did, firing aimlessly into the sky. But maybe I was the only one. The Jerries were the enemy, after all, and we had to hate them. There was even one man who kept a score. It made me feel a traitor, when they talked of how the war was being won and me not doing my bit. Even John Allen that we called Long John, I couldn't tell him about it. He was a tall man with a mimic's gift. He had this loud voice that could bend and stretch, and his face would bend and stretch along with it. He could do lugubrious or hilarious or the two at once. He was paired up with another tall bloke and they'd do turns together. Once they did train rides. Long John came from Devon and the other chap was from the Lake District. They'd both spent a lot of time on trains, or else they made it up. The game was about who could come up with the most memorable train ride. Uttoxeter to Netheravon, Long John would go. Stops at Pickleford and Jim's Bush and Cowleaze. There's more flowers growing on the station at Jim's Bush than in Kew Gardens in summer, he says, and Pickleford has got seventeen pubs in a circle round a duck pond. That's nothing, goes the other one. The daffodils in April are so thick round the line from Castle Mary to Plump-hampton that the driver won't go more than five miles an hour for fear of blowing them over. On the long bend by Fipenny Small, the school-kids jump down from the train, dash over the field and catch the train again on the other side. They all come to school with yellow backsides from the pollen. Long John and the other chap could go on for hours with such stuff. It sounds odd saying it, but I was jealous of those two. I wished it was me that was Long John's special mate. Like being back at school when it mattered who was whose best friend. They both died the same day. Good thing, I suppose, because I don't know how they would have done without each other.'

'All this isn't getting us anywhere, Jack,' said Charles Yeoman.

'It's got us at least as far as Plumphampton,' said Jack.

By the fire, Maggie Fox sat still, with tears running down her face.

'Supper's ready,' Mrs Dooley announced briskly. 'If you need a wash, there's a basin and a jug in the washroom next to the scullery.

The closet's outside, at the end of the corridor. Take a lamp. You come and give me a hand, m'dear,' she said to Maggie Fox. She took up a lamp and led the way to the scullery.

'You'll be wanting to have a wash,' she said to the girl as they went out. 'That's the washroom on the right. Leave the lamp there after you've finished, then come and fetch some dishes from the scullery.'

In the washroom, the lamplight made a circle in the gloom. There was a smell of soap and when Maggie ran her hand over the towel, it was freshly laundered. She poured water into the basin and washed the salt tears from her face and the grime of the road from her hands and neck. The schoolchildren at Plumphampton arrive in spring with yellow bottoms, she thought. There are seventeen pubs round the pond in … where was it … Jim's Bush? She smiled through fresh tears. Back in the scullery, Mrs Dooley was busy with dishes and cutlery.

'There's a tray for the dishes and watch the step as you go through,' she said. 'Put the dishes on the hearth and lay the table for five.'

In the corridor, Maggie met Charles going to wash.

'Don't let him upset you, Margaret,' he said. 'I'll go with him to Dover in the morning and he'll be back with his regiment the next day.'

'He fires in the air, he said.'

'Don't you believe it. Jack's a better shot than I am.'

This much was true, she thought. Charles was always just wide of the mark.

Jack was at the table, looking up at her as she came in. He must have seen her tears, because something like guilt crossed his face and something like tenderness came after. For a moment they stared at each other and in that moment she saw that he loved her, and not like a brother loves. He looked quickly away because of what she had seen and then he was inspecting the table and shifting his chair and asking himself what on earth he meant by that look which he had no right to give, a man condemned for running away.

When she had put out the dishes and fetched the cutlery and the pickle and the head of cheese and the bowl of Stubbard apples, she sat down next to him, on his right. She wanted to be close enough so that his hand on the table might brush against hers, she wanted to catch the scent of his blue-black hair, she wanted to watch his fingers as they broke bread, she wanted to feel his eyes light on her.

Mrs Dooley was salting and stirring. Rich whiffs of beef stew rose from the stirred pot. Mrs Dooley drew forth a taster, blew on it, sipped and got busy with a very long ladle.

'You'll be needing rooms for the night, I take it,' she said. 'I'll set fires in two rooms above here for the men. The lass can take the spare bed in my room if there's no objection.'

There was none, and not much talk of any kind round the Blackfriars' table, as if the rule of the monks endured still. For a while Bill Bate looked at his food without touching it, but in the end he skewered a potato with his fork and that went down so he tried a carrot and a parsnip and after that it all followed as it should, to the last drop of broth. When the landlady returned from upstairs, she refilled whatever dishes were empty, without asking, and the second round went the way of the first, because Mrs Dooley's hotpot was not easily refused by hungry men. Only Maggie declined another helping, but Jack Yeoman's every mouthful was feeding her too.

Mrs Dooley began clearing the dishes and Maggie got up to help. When she took Jack's dish, she saw that the Skull One lay there on the table. He'd turned them to the Skull One beside his plate, she thought. He must have had his hand cupped over them even at the moment when their eyes had met. It made her suddenly angry, the way he guarded this ominous sign. Any sane man would have ... but what would any sane man have done? The options were not six, but only two: go back to France and die there, stay in Dorset and die here. Either way it was the skull. Maggie Fox did not believe in flight. She could not imagine Jack Yeoman hiding out for the rest of the war, with a new moustache in London or as an itinerant farm worker among the hills of the north.

'Out of my way, gents,' Mrs Dooley said in sudden haste. 'Finish your drinks by the fire. There's the table to be cleared and the dishes to be seen to and my cats to be fed or they'll be under our feet to remind us.'

'Would there be a bone for my dog, Missus?' Cockler asked, and she said that there were a couple of good ones in the pot if he cared to scoop them out.

Cockler went to the pot and took up Mrs Dooley's ladle.

'Your ladle's longer than my arm, Mrs Dooley,' he said.

'Long enough to get to the bottom of things,' she said.

Cockler extracted two dripping bones from the pot and set them on the hearth.

'There's a tin dish at the back of the fireplace,' Mrs Dooley said. 'Shoo the cats out of the barn. Otherwise they'll be sniffing after the dog's food.'

'I'll look to the horses at the same time,' Cockler said, and Bill Bate said he'd step out too to see if the storm was like to blow off before the night. They went out together, letting in a squall of wind and rain. The wind ran round the room buffeting the flames of the lamps and chasing the shadows up the walls.

The women took out the dishes, and the two brothers were alone by the fire.

'I suggest we turn in, Jack old man,' said Charles. 'We'll need an early start in the morning.'

'We're sharing a room then.'

'We'll have a talk before we sleep. Like the old days. Remember?'

'Talk about what, Charles? Skull Six?'

'You must forget that nonsense with the dice, Jack. Alright, so they were a gift from father. You know that father had his ... eccentricities. They're what you said yourself, a kind of game.'

'I left them on the table,' Jack said, getting up to retrieve them.

But the table was cleared, and the dice weren't there.

'You pocketed the dice!' he accused his brother.

'I have no idea where your damned dice are,' Charles said.

Jack looked under the table and around the floor. He marched into the kitchen, where Maggie and Mrs Dooley were washing the dishes, demanding to know what had happened to the dice. Maggie Fox rounded on him furiously. Who did he think he was, accusing them of taking his stupid dice, accusing *her* in fact, since he couldn't seriously be pointing a finger at the landlady. Nobody but him would want to have anything whatever to do with the dice, she said, and no doubt he'd find them kicked into a corner where they belonged.

'What do you want with them now?' she said, 'What more do you want with those pointless fribbles, which anybody in their right mind would have thrown out with the rubbish a long time ago? Good riddance to them, I say, and you can leave us to get on with our work.'

He stood in the doorway of the kitchen, trying to find an answer. She'd never spoken to him like that, and he knew, oddly, that it was connected with the look they had exchanged before, as if some old, familiar barrier between them had been lifted, revealing ... revealing what? Something he had no heart for now. He turned away from the kitchen and back into the taproom, where the door jerked open to admit Cockler and Bill Bate and once more the shadows cast by lamp-light and firelight leapt madly up the walls as a corner of the storm flew in from the outside.

Mrs Dooley came in from the kitchen. 'You gentlemen must make yourselves at home,' she said. 'If you want more beer, we can see to the score in the morning. I'll show you where the rooms are and you can turn in when you please. I'll look after the lass and see to it that she gets a good night's rest, which is what she needs.'

'I wouldn't want to dirty any linen for the sake of a night,' Bill Bate said, 'and Cockler's of the same mind. Besides I don't have the coin to pay my way and wouldn't feel right for anyone to settle it for me. So I'll just lay down on one of these benches here and thank you for a blanket if you've got one to spare.'

'Same goes for me,' Cockler said.

'As you wish,' said the landlady. 'There's a room each for the captain and his brother, then. The fires are lit so you might as well use them. Follow me, Captain, and I'll show you where they are.'

'Cockler, did you pick up my dice?' Jack demanded, when they'd gone.

'Swallowed 'em down with my last sup of ale,' said Cockler, 'just like you'd do with any other bitter pills. Thought they might cure me from my habit of thinking too much.'

'You don't take me seriously, do you?' Jack said.

'I take you seriously enough,' said Cockler coming up to him, taking him by the arm and speaking quietly into his ear. 'I like you the better, Johnny, because things matter to you. But I don't like this business of the dice, because six is not all the options there are, and rolling dice is a fool's way to choose between them. Listen to me, John. There's the option of climbing in my wagon a bit later and hiding out until I set off tomorrow before it's light, and once we're on the road, there'll be other options, you can be sure. Or there's the option of saying yes to your brother and once you're on the way to Dover in your uniform again, why you can get off anywhere you please and start again, without involving your girl and your brother, just quietly and deliberately like I do myself. You haven't learnt, Johnny, that it's fair enough to say yes meaning no if there's a purpose to it. Six options be damned! I've got more options as to how to pick my nose on the quiet.'

'The die is cast,' Jack said.

'Uncast it.' Cockler slapped him on the shoulder and walked off towards the fire to get warm and see if there was life in the flagon. It was the first time in Cockler's life that he was invited to help himself in a public house.

146

Chapter Nine

The Margarets

The Margarets knew the secret of the sixth mood, called humility or earthiness. It is controlled by the sixth of the planets known to the ancients, Earth itself, and signified by the cross.

(Louis Yeoman, *Journals*)

MRS Dooley's room was in a separate wing of the house, divided from the main building by a covered walk. Then there was a winding corridor, a set of stairs and another corridor still. The air was cold and the floorboards muttered. Maggie Fox thought of the landlady making her nightly way to bed along these creaking galleries and wondered at her choice of bedroom. The light of Mrs Dooley's oil lamp bobbed and flickered. The rain pelted against the windows. The lamplight was reflected in the glass of the windows, and above it the faces of the women danced fleetingly across the panes as if made of something less substantial than flesh.

'I live so far off,' said Mrs Dooley as she opened the door to her room, 'because I'm a woman running an inn for men, and although these men are a gentle crowd for the most part and would no more lift a finger against me than against their own little ones, too much drink can make a monster of a mild man, and it's better that the place where I sleep should not be guessed.'

Maggie followed her into the room and found to her surprise that it was the warmest room in the mazy house.

'I like to keep this room warm,' Mrs Dooley said, 'and my cats like it too. One or two of them may curl up here all day, but these are the ones that will be out and about most of the night. There are others that use this room after dark. Like that one there,' she said pointing to a shape on the chair by the window. 'They are particular about the company they keep and sometimes they squabble. That one's Punch, and the others are Pop and Grog and Toddy and Malt and Stout. Stout grew up skinny, but he's the best ratter of the six.'

'How do they get in and out?'

'Dooley made a hole in the corner cubbert and the door of the next room stays ajar. The cats come and go as they please and the room keeps warm. Sit yourself down by the fire, m'dear, and I'll make us a cup of tea. That'll be your bed over there. The girl who helps me keep this place going sleeps there sometimes if there's a storm or snow or something that makes her afraid. You mustn't mind if Punch curls up next to you during the night, because that's what he likes to do when there's a visitor.'

The dark journey by corridors and stairways had set a great distance between themselves and the rest of the company. Mrs Dooley's warm, comfortable room was a world apart. It was faintly familiar to Maggie, as if she had seen it pictured in a book of nursery rhymes, or as if she had once slept here as a child.

'Some say we remember things from previous lives,' Mrs Dooley said. 'I don't go for that. If we've had a dozen lives already, this very one loses what makes it special is my way of looking at it.'

'You must get through a lot of logs, Mrs Dooley,' Maggie said, unwilling just then to grapple with such weighty matters.

'Logs are a fair kind of payment in these parts. It's a rare family that can't spare a basketful of sticks, and a cartload of stumps is within the means of some. So I take my fees in timber as often as not, though also in milk or eggs or mushrooms, or an armful of hay if that's all there is to be had. But I always take a fee, even from the poorest, because that's the rule and there's a good reason for it.'

'Fee for what?'

'For my calling, m'dear,' said Mrs Dooley. She had the kettle over the fire now, raking the ashes under it to excite the heat.

'As landlady?'

'To run an inn is no kind of calling. I speak of my real craft.'

'You are a healer,' said Maggie Fox, suddenly enlightened.

The older woman nodded. 'People come to me with their aches and pains and worse. Mostly my teapot can come up with something to shift the inner moods. Folk take away a few herbs or roots or powders, and after that it's up to their own teapots. There's nothing like a person's own pot.'

Her own was a stout black one, with a design in brushstrokes of red. Maggie went closer and by the light of the fire she made out a red dragon coiling the girth of the black teapot. Below the spout was the dragon's head with its tail in its mouth.

'It looks Chinese,' Maggie said.

'Does it, m'dear? It's a homegrown dragon nonetheless, drawn by my own hand and no other. Tonight it'll brew up a little something to help you sleep. These men have been crowding you with their fights and nonsenses, and you could do with a bit of distance from that.'

'I wish it were nonsense.'

'There's nonsense clinging to it is what I mean, like mud to a boot.

Makes it heavy and changes its shape.'

'It's his dice you're talking about.'

'They're not his dice, m'dear.'

Maggie was by the fire watching the flames. Mrs Dooley's words came from behind her, and the girl sensed a proprietal tone, an admonition.

'You know about the dice,' she said.

'In the hands of a healer, the dice can help with healing. In the hands of a soldier, they cannot help with soldiering. In the hands of your young man, they have become … '

'An addiction.'

'A distortion was the word I was going for. Those dice can twist things. Jack Yeoman cast the dice at the friar's table like a conjurer's trick. This is not a healing but a misleading. Look, Punch has moved to your bed already. How does he know that you're staying the night? That's a bigger mystery than the dice, or the same mystery put another way, perhaps. There's nobody ever dinged the bottom out of time.'

'What happened to your husband, Mrs Dooley?' Maggie asked.

'Dooley? I was never married to Dooley. He worked for me for a year. He could turn his hand to anything, Dooley. Timber, stone or brick, hinges and handles and hooks. It was all the same to him. He even stopped the taproom fireplace from smoking, and he did it with a few bricks in the chimney. I never did work out where exactly he put them. There's still patches of wet in the walls, but there's never a tile missing from the roofs and not a window but closes fast.'

'But you're Mrs Dooley. It says so on the board.'

'It's like having a bedroom a little way off and a ladle long enough for supping with the devil. When Dooley was around I let people think he was my man, and when he'd finished the work and left I borrowed his name, which he wouldn't have minded being the sweet, clever man he was. It's not so very hard a thing for a woman to have her freedom in a world managed by men, but it needs a little care, like anything worth having.'

Maggie Fox nodded. She'd grown up among three wilful men.

'Now that you know the secret of my husband who never was, you can leave off calling me Mrs Dooley and call me by my given name, which is the same as yours near enough. Marguerita. Tomorrow when there's folk about, you can use Mrs Dooley, to save trouble.'

She made the tea, first warming the pot, then adding dried leaves from tins on the chimneybreast. 'There's lavender and hypericum, hops and valerian, together with a few dried mushrooms which I shall point out to you one day perhaps. It's the combination that counts, and you mustn't think you can get the same effect by leaving one out. It's an old recipe and has to be followed exactly.'

Another brew, Maggie thought. 'I won't have tea, thank you,' she said.

'Don't you be frightened of the dragon teapot, m'dear. There's only wholesome drinks come from that spout. The worst that can happen is that you'll sleep a little late in the morning.'

'He may leave early tomorrow, and I'll be here not knowing where he has gone.'

'Let him go off if that's what he does. He'll see more clearly on his own and without the dice to muddle his thinking.'

'It was you that took the dice,' Maggie said.

The older woman poured a cup of tea from the pot and passed it to the girl who set it down without drinking. 'The dice are stubborn and tricky,' she said. 'They need to be learned.'

'Can they tell me where I will find Jack in the morning?'

'The dice tell moods and signs, not hunt-my-thimble.'

Marguerita pulled the dice from the pocket of her apron and placed them by the dragon teapot on the hearth.

'I know the six moods but Jack Yeoman does not,' she said. 'The difference between fate and chance, his father told him, but he could not grasp the meaning of that and chance is all he got.'

'What moods? Why six?'

'Mood is our word for the humours of people or places, or subtle influences borne by winds and gathered in fogs. Six because six is our number and the number of faces on the dice, which were fashioned in the land of the six rivers.'

'Each river has a mood?'

'Certainly. But what's important is that the dice spin to the moods of this lap of land and no other. Then there are times and seasons. In midsummer, the dice are idle and little can be learned from them. Daylight too robs them of some of their virtues. At dusk and dawn they can show more, and on certain days of the year, which can be easily guessed. The full moon, the solstice, the equinox. The moods gather and shift, like currents of air. They cast their influences, for good or ill. This time of All Hallows is when the year turns finally to winter. It is the death of the spirit born in spring and we register its death, no matter how gross the tangle of our self-deceptions. There are similar seasons in people's lives, when the dark forces gather and demand a fee. Times of judgement, which people call crisis. On the eve of All Hallows, it is said that the spirits of the dead are abroad. Some lie in fear during this night, with strings of garlic hung on their doors and their fires banked up with oak logs. Some paint crosses on their garden gates and leave their bibles open at favourite passages. Women of my stripe have been taken and burned on this day. It was the time for the hunting of innocent folk on no more evidence than a black cat and a wallet of herbs. One woman was taken for what she painted on the timbers of her fireplace. The ghost of such deeds lives on, Maggie, and this is revealed by the Margarets' dice.'

'You frighten me,' said the girl.

'I do so, m'dear. You can't take a proper step without the fear, but it's not boundless, even though it may appear that way sometimes. Don't lose your way in it and it won't drown you. It's only fear and it can do nothing more than make afraid.'

'I'm afraid for Jack.'

'Fear gives you an edge and sometimes the healer must make a cut. I knew the knucklebones once upon a time, but I never got to like them nor they me. But it may be different with you, Maggie. The dice don't belong to Jack Yeoman, as I said. They belong to you. You'll not understand the why's and wherefore's, but the dice are your very own.'

The cat got up and stretched itself before curling up on the bed again. A sharp blast of wind drove a flurry of raindrops against the window and the branches of a creeper outside were flung against the glass.

'Do I want them, though?' Maggie said.

'Want or not, they are yours and you must learn them.'

Maggie looked at them where they lay on the grate. The red die showed the cross, on the white was the one.

'What does Cross One mean?' she said.

'The cross is where earth meets heaven and the soul meets the body and where the son of man met his death. The place where suffering meets joy. It is called humility.'

'Where is the joy in death?'

'Where is the joy without it? You know the story perhaps of the man who prayed for eternal life. Prayed day in and day out, because he could not abide the thought of death. At last, God answered his prayers and told the man that he would never die. *The relief of immortality*! He travelled where he wished, did what he wanted to do and avoided what he did not. He came to live in a fair land with a calm sea and trees full of fruit, among people who like him would never know death. He lived there for some years, perhaps not as many as you might think, until tedium cast its shadow. Even the plump fruit became tedious, and the sea without storms. At last he prayed that the gift of death be returned to him. The *gift* of death, he said now. God heard his prayer and sent a great bird to fetch him back to the world of death. During the flight, the bird was battered by winds and dropped him into the angry waves, and he began to drown. ''Lord! Lord!'' he cried. ''Save me!'' God heard him for the third time and plucked him from the waves, asking him where he would be set down, in the world of life-without-death or in the world of life. There would be no further choice, God said. ''Then give me the world of life,'' the man said. And God dropped him again.'

'He died.'

'Then or later.'

'Cross One, it says. What is the one?'

'The white die points. Here it may point to you, because you are one, or to this moment, which is the now. Cross One will often mean this now.'

Maggie took up the dice.

'Perhaps I can use them to help Jack,' she said.

'An hour ago they were mere fribbles and now they are your little helpers. They are neither, and you cannot *use* them. You can only ask them what you want to know. Let them learn the feel of your hands. Get them warm and lively and when you're ready throw them six times without stopping. Don't be afraid of them. They have no power but what you find in them. Does the weatherglass make the weather?'

Maggie shook them in her hands. The faint chinking of the dice one against the other had a reassuring quality.

'Tip them from hand to hand but don't drop them,' Marguerita said.

Maggie obeyed, cautiously at first. It was something like shaping pastry. As they turned in her hands, she glimpsed the tumbling faces of the red die. Sword and circle. Pillar and cross.

'How can there be only thirty-six options?' she asked.

'The dice are thrown six times I said. If you learned arithmetic at school, you can multiply. Six times thirty-six. Is that enough for you?'

'Two hundred and sixteen,' she said. 'It still seems very little next to … next to infinity.'

'Leave infinity out of it. How many diseases are there? How many cures? How many plants growing in the Dorset hills and vales?'

'How can you remember the meaning of thirty-six signs?'

'If you taught a class of thirty-six children, would you not soon learn their names and their faces and something of their natures?'

One of the dice spilled from Maggie's hands and she caught it one-handed before it hit the floor.

'Don't drop them!' Marguerita said. 'When the dice are woken, ask them what you will and cast them six times, calling them aloud.'

Maggie continued tipping the dice until they grew faster and lighter and their chinking pleasant and rhythmical like a brook over a pebble bank. There came the feeling of something running through her hands, a stream connecting her to another place. She tried to shape a question in her mind – what would happen and where and how could she help – but what came out were three blunt words: 'Will Jack die?' and the dice answered bluntly. Skull One, they said, and she did not pick them up.

'You must complete the sentence,' Marguerita said.

'*Must*? The dice are mine, you said, and I shall do with them as I wish. I can take them to the window and throw them out and you cannot stop me. Skull One. What can be clearer than that?'

'Skull is a reminder of mortality and we are all mortal. The one is a pointer, but you do not know at whom it points. Perhaps at the man who died this afternoon. Who was that man?'

'We lost our way in the woods and came to his house on the marsh,' said Maggie. 'There was a fog thick around his house. He was dressed as a priest, but he was no priest. He was a dangerous, deceitful person and Jack couldn't see it. He made me tea which poisoned me. The next day he threatened me with a gun and Bate killed him. But it was not of him that I asked the dice.'

'A healer cannot always prevent death,' Marguerita said quietly.

'I am not a healer. I am a ... I am a woman who loves a man.'

'I know it, m'dear, yet your love cannot make everything right. But now you must complete the sentence.'

'Why not cast the dice yourself? Perhaps they came here for you.'

'Some has dice and some has teapots. The land itself has moods and you know this for yourself. Places that elate and places that depress. Places that shut in and places that set free. This place where we now sit is built over the site of druid circles, a place of gathering and the strength to be found in circles. The monks arrived with the cross and built a chapel, but 'tis said that it was not a good place for them and brought them hardship and sorrow. When I came, I had Dooley bring six stones to make the square hearth a circle. My hearth is round and the dining-table is round and so is the dragon that girdles my teapot. I keep six cats and there are six barrels in the taproom. The proper sign for *The Duntish Rings* is Circle Six, which is the sign of reunion and completion. The stone circle is the mood of this place, which will not change except if the land itself changes. Look at the fire.'

The flames had eaten away the middle part of the logs, leaving an almost perfect ring of charred wood, with glowing embers at its heart.

'Nothing strange, you will say, in the burning away of the centre leaving a circle of wood. The fire and the circle are connected and the ring of fire is an old sign. But I have never seen fires make such perfect circles as they do in this very room, night after night. I do not want the dice, child. I have other things around me.'

'Jack threw the Circle Six after the priest died.'

'Then it was the Circle Six that brought you to the *Rings*. But there were only five of you who came. It's the priest that should be the sixth. Tell me more of this man. You spoke of a brew he gave you to drink.'

'It was sage, he said, and chamomile, and something more.'

'What more, child? It's the *more* that counts.'

'Some seeds. A thorn. Black thorn. No. Sweet thorn.'

'Thornapple.'

'Yes. Thornapple. It was thornapple.'

'Indeed it was. And where did you go when you drank this brew?'

'There was a sensation of riding away. More like being ridden away. Over great distances at great speed. But all the time, I was lying helpless on the couch.'

'And you stayed there till morning.'

'No. Jack woke me and we left. I must have fallen from my horse. The priest told me his dog found me on the marsh.'

'The dog was black and white?'

'Yes, if it makes any difference.'

'Regrettably it does, child. The dog had a sharp white flash through one eye, perhaps?'

Maggie nodded. 'The dog found me and the priest carried me to his house, he said. I remember nothing of that.'

'Where did you wake in the morning?'

'I woke on a high bed when it was still dark. I took the horses and left. Even when I left, the fog was deep.'

'Yes, yes, a dead fog.'

'I remember now when I first woke. It seemed as if I had just landed there, high on the bed over the deep sea of fog.'

'The thornapple ride don't properly end for a day or three, m'dear.'

'The horses were in the yard and I rode off to look for Jack. The priest came after me.'

'He will come here tonight.'

'But he is dead. Bate killed him.'

'He will come tonight. It was in the sentence of the dice. Circle Six, it read. The priest is the sixth.'

'Why should it not be you, the sixth?'

'The dice cannot catch me. Nor I them. It is the priest.'

'Why will he come?'

'I have heard tell of a priest and his dog. The folk who come to me with their ills bring their talk too. As for the house on the marsh, it has a history for us. Yes, I know of the so-called priest, and maybe I know what manner of man he is. Did he see the dice?'

'He stole them from Jack's pocket. I saw him do it.'

'He wants the dice, and that cannot be allowed. There will be no sleep for you tonight. It's fortunate that you have not touched your tea, if fortunate is the word. The priest will come early or late and if he is who I think he is, he will not come by the front door.'

'He will think that Jack has the dice.'

'He will know who has them.'

'Then I shall give him the accursed things and there's an end to it.'

'Then there will be worse to come.'

'Worse? Worse than *what*? Worse than Jack deserting and the army coming after him? Worse than Charles forcing him back to the trenches to be killed in his turn?'

'If you learn the ways of the dice, they can protect you. With them in your hand, the priest whenever and however he comes will not be able to touch you. Listen to me carefully. You will set them to Cross Six and you will close them in the palms of your two hands with your fingers upwards so that if you open them the cross and the six will be showing. You will hold out your hands towards him and you will say in your clear voice: "By the power of the Margarets' cross, begone from me." And he will have to go. To say it once, without faltering, is enough. But you can repeat it over and over if it helps you.'

'If he comes, I will give them to him and be rid of them.'

'You cannot turn your back on the dice. If you hand them over to an evil one, he will do evil with them and some of that evil will return to you. It is not only this unfinished sentence that may send your man to the gallows or to a grave in France. There will be other sentences, and those too you will be a part of. There was another man you loved, was there not, Margaret Fox?'

'How do you know it?'

'It is my craft to divine such things, m'dear. He was Jack Yeoman's father who died?'

She nodded.

'A man who makes a gift to his son who is going to war and may never return does not give him fribbles. Jack's father knew the value of the dice. You must trust him now as you did when he was alive. That is what we mean by honouring the dead, child. It is known to all true peoples through all times. If we do not honour the dead, they lived their lives in vain.'

'Then I will do what I must,' Maggie said.

'Not everything belongs to the realm of the dice – but in those things that do there are simple rules. The Cross Six is a charm for the

160

Margarets. Believe it. With the Cross Six in your hands, you are protected. The cross should be in your left hand and the six in the right. Memorise this and practise it because the moment will come unexpectedly. Always the moment of judgement comes unexpectedly. It follows that your attention must not wander. The attention of a Margaret must never wander. Remember too that in this realm of the dice, not everything is what it seems. Therefore expect anything. Predict nothing.'

'You are saying that I may not recognise him when he comes.'

'You will recognise him, even if his form is not what you expect. So I say: expect nothing and there will come a moment when you will know.'

'I am very afraid,' said the girl. 'Won't you stay with me?'

'If I stay with you, he will wait until I am gone. We can put off the moment if you wish. But it is better that he should come tonight when you are prepared and when I am at hand than tomorrow night or the night after when your guard is down and I will perhaps be far off.'

The older woman picked up one of the lamps and made towards the door.

'You're not going already?'

'I am,' Marguerita said, her hand on the door.

'But I've forgotten the words!' Maggie called out.

'You have not indeed,' said Marguerita and left the room, closing the door behind her.

By the cross begone. But it was longer than that. By the Margarets' cross begone from me. Was that right? By the Margarets' cross begone from me. Still something missing. And then she had it. By the power of the Margarets' cross, begone from me. She murmured the charm repeatedly until it lay ready on her lips. Which hand for which dice? Cross in the right hand, surely. No, for it had surprised her. Left for the cross. Right for the six. Get them ready. Palms upward. Cross lying face up on the left hand. Six face up on the right. Close the fists. Okay. How would he come? Bursting in at the doorway, insolent, maleficent. Or the window. Surely not. It was high off the ground. Could he fly, this sorcerer? The word came unbidden. In at the window. Worse than a sudden battering at the door. Expect anything. Predict nothing. The chimney then. Or not a manshape at all. A bird, a bat, a beast … Predict nothing, she told herself. She opened her clenched fists to check the sign. Cross Six. If you believe it, it's true. But what if you don't believe? I don't believe! And if I don't, it won't. Believe it, know it, she said. The cat lay quietly on the bed that was to have been her own. She was glad of it. The cat was an ally. Where had she read … how did she know … cats were psychic, that strange word, like metal against metal. They were ... alert to things, including the unseen. The cat would sense it if something were about to happen. She would give a sign.

'Punch, Punch,' she called out, and the cat looked indifferently over one shoulder before curling up again. The company of the cat made her feel stronger. She recited her words once more. She had them now. Once more she checked the sign she carried in her hands. She listened for a footfall on the corridor, a sound coming from outside, up the wall, in the branches of the creeper. How thick was the trunk of that creeper? Surely not thick enough to support the weight of a man. But a lesser creature? What exactly had Marguerita said? A different form.

162

Not the form you would expect. A disguise? The cat lifted its head, cocked its ears and in a whisker was off the bed onto the floor and disappearing through the gap in the corner.

Why so sudden? The cat had heard something. Her ears had cocked. But there was no sound from beyond the walls of the room. The silence was complete. She heard something I couldn't. So many sounds going on out of my range. We hear only the middle notes. Can't catch the tiny high whines and tinks, the muffled thuds and fluffs. Bugs abroad and small birds in flight and bat waves going and millions on millions of dust motes travelling on currents of air. Batwaves, what's that? Batwaves indeed!

The cat reappeared in the corner, whisking its tail.

'Come on, Punch,' she whispered, glad at its return.

The cat stood in the corner looking round. It was not Punch this time, she saw. This one was darker with a broader head. A tom. Grog? Pop? Toddy? Stout? She called the names in turn. There was a name she had forgotten. Six cats, she had said. Punch, Grog, Pop, Toddy, Stout and … Malt. Maybe this one was Malt. Sounded dark, somehow.

'Malt! Malt!' she whispered.

The cat came further into the middle of the room, looking round, tail twitching.

'Something wrong with your eye is there, Malt?' the girl whispered. One of its eyes was half-closed. The lid seemed swollen. 'Something get in your eye, did it? Come here and let me look.'

The cat came closer. It seemed nervous and when the girl put out her hand to it, it crouched tensely, its left eye almost closed.

'Don't be afraid of me,' Maggie said, holding out her hand. 'Let me

163

look at that eye of yours.'

It was the other eye she should have been looking at. In the other eye was a bold glaring wildness and the body was crouched not from fear but to strike and the cat's body flew at her from the floor with the claws extended straight at her face and it was too late for charms or mantras all she could do was to fling her arms in front of her face and she felt the blades of the cat's claws on the flesh of her forearm. Her fingers opened and the dice dropped to the floor. 'Begone!' she screamed, but the dice had fallen, the words were wrong, the moment was wrong, the cat clung to her arm and struck at her face. She bent her head away and closed her eyes, shielding them with her free hand, and shouted out because she knew not what else '*By the power of the Margarets' cross, begone from me!*'

At once the claws let go her flesh, there was a screech and then the noise of heavy steps scampering over the floor towards the door which opened suddenly and shut with a bang. Later, when she remembered this scene, what was dreadful was this scampering of feet which were not the paws of a cat nor yet the feet of a human being but something unthinkable between the two. And although she persuaded herself that she must have been looking the other way, it was not so, and she knew it was not so. She had been looking directly towards the door and had seen it open and bang shut but there was nothing, no shape of animal or human between her and the door. There was only the sudden swift passage of the scampering limbs.

She had learned one lesson and quite forgotten the other more important one, but she was a Margaret after all and whether by chance or by fate the dice had fallen to the floor showing Cross Six. There was a sound by the door and she watched terrified as the handle turned, but it was Marguerita come back, her face gone pale and her composure fled. Maggie Fox was incapable of speech, but the Cross Six told part of the story and as for the rest of it, Marguerita held that the girl had been panicked by one of the tomcats, and that was the story that Maggie herself chose to believe, for the alternatives were beyond her imagining.

Chapter Ten

Pillar One

The pillar is Hermes, Thoth, Balder of Broadblink; the message and the messenger, the seed and the sower. (Louis Yeoman, *Journals*)

JACK YEOMAN lay between clean dry sheets under warm blankets and watched the flames of the fire dwindle and listened to the rain on the window panes. He did not wish to sleep. He wanted to enjoy this rare comfort all the long night. But the fire needed logs. This meant emerging from under the blankets, and like the frog in the pot Jack put off the moment.

There was a rap at the door and Charles let himself in.

'Are you awake Jack?' he said.

'I am.'

'There's something I want to talk over with you, and I thought I'd better not put it off.'

'Sit yourself down then, brother. Put some wood on the fire first. And no talk of the army or the war.'

'No, no. None of that. That's all settled,' Charles said. He fed a couple of logs to the fire before sitting down on the edge of the bed. For a while the two brothers watched the fire in silence.

'I have some news for you, Jack,' Charles said. 'Good news. I'm sure you'll think of it as good news. May come as a bit of a surprise, though. What with … the way things have been before.'

'Don't sit on it then, like a hen on an addled egg. Let's hear your news.'

'I'm going to ask Margaret to marry me.'

Jack kept his mouth shut for fear of blurting something he couldn't retract.

'It won't be what you'd call a love match,' Charles said. 'Margaret's been like a sister to us. But she and I have been together a lot while you've been away. Breakfast together in the kitchen. Supper together. We understand each other, I think. And there's her own future to consider. She's a woman now. She can stay on at Manston House as before, but I don't know that she'd want that. I mean, there could be another woman in the house later. If we get married, everything will be easier for both of us. A partnership. Children.'

'You haven't spoken to her.'

'To tell the truth, old man, I was going to wait until you got back. Wouldn't have wanted to go ahead without you knowing about it first. You'll give the idea your blessing, won't you, old chap?'

'I wish you wouldn't call me old chap.'

'But what about it? Good scheme for everyone concerned, don't you think?'

Absolutely not. She doesn't love you. You don't love her. It's ridiculous. But he had no right to say such things. He was a man condemned. If he died, would he leave behind him nothing but a dead brother's ban?

'You'd better ask Maggie,' he said at last.

'Of course. Of course. No knowing what she'll say. She might find the idea absurd.'

She might, Jack thought.

'But you'll not stand in our way, at least?' Charles said.

'How could I? Why would I? If you want to marry Maggie and she says yes, what objection could I have?'

'I knew you'd see it like that, old man. When the war's over and you're back with us, we can make some proper plans. You can set up for yourself at Lower Farm, perhaps, as you suggested.'

First marry Maggie and then move me out, he thought. He's got the whole thing planned. But why the devil should I mind? I'll be dead anyway.

'That's right, Charles. You do what's best,' he said.

Maggie would say no. Surely she would say no.

'Thanks, old chap. Children, you know. I've been thinking that Manston House needs children.' Charles got up from the bed. 'I'll throw another log on before I go,' he said. 'Keep the place warm for you. Sleep well.'

But all the comfort was gone from the room and Jack lay awake much later when there was a further knock at his door.

'I'm awake, Charles,' he said.

The door opened and Maggie Fox came in.

'Something frightened me, Jack,' she said.

'Come in, dearest Maggie. Come here and sit with me.' Jack pulled himself up and made to get out of bed.

'Don't get up, Jack. I'll just perch here on the edge.'

She sat on the edge of the bed, and when he thought that she might be cold, she lay down beside him, covering herself with one of his blankets, and later when this didn't seem to either of them quite con-venient, she slipped in beside him under the bedclothes and he put his arm round her because the bed was narrow, and whether it was the narrowness of the bed or some other thing, they lay close together, like spoons, and whispered together in case they might be heard or because whispering suited what they had to tell each other.

Jack woke very early in the morning, but Maggie slept on, and slept still when Jack kissed her brow, quietly opened the door and left.

Rouse Cockler, he thought. Off together with wagon and dog. Why involve Cockler? Because Cockler was *lucky*. But if Cockler got up, Bate would be up. Dog would be up. Horse would need harnessing to the wagon. The whole house would be up. He went quietly through the taproom and let himself out. The priest's advice: he travels fastest who travels alone. The priest had travelled fast alright. All the way over. Not saved by his own wit. The day before, all that stuff about how to save yourself; the next day, *paf*! Gone.

In the barn, Cockler's dog came up, sniffing, wagging his tail. They don't forget like we do. One sniff. It's a friend. No enemy at least. Which horse? The priest's piebald. If I take the bay mare, the black one would kick up a fuss. Besides, the squire would have people looking out for his horses. Let Bate return them.

He threw a handful of grain to the squire's horses and saddled the stallion who postured in virile mood but made less fuss than he'd expected. He led the horse into the yard and got the barn door shut behind them, but Cockler's dog had come out and stayed out. He rode off quickly.

There's only Charles to come after you, on the bike. So take to the fields. Stay off the roads. Work out the route as you go along. He turned left along the road and took the first gateway, passing under the blackness of a great tree. From this tree came the first birdsong of the day. Blackbird. Earlybird. In the east, was the glimmer of dawn.

He was headed north, more or less. One field led to another. Two hours to Sherborne? More maybe by the fields. Police had been told. Dorchester might be better. Police there too, and the army, but still less chance of being caught. Bigger place. Not so ... nosey. But perhaps I want to get caught?

Sherborne was where he went to school for five dull, painful years. On Sundays he cycled home to get away. Cycled back again in the evening with tears in his eyes. Whole town smelled of school and church. Town and gown, they quipped, but the place was mostly gown. Gowns and straw hats, for decoration only. Hats chipped if you threw them, broke if you sat on them. The brittle badges of class. Pack them off to the Somme, let them wear them there. Stroll up and down in no-man's land in straw boaters – 'Just studying the war, old bean!' Scripture classes by war beaks. And it came to pass that God did visit a horrible pestilation on the land of Somme. The men of Somme were cut down and cut off. The land was laid waste. The limbs of the men of Somme lay scattered in the fields and the fowls of the air fed on the limbs of the men of Somme. Great was the lamenting of the women of the men of Somme, and great was the feasting of the fowls of the air on the bones of the men and the women of Somme. And Somme begat Golgotha. No. Golgotha begat the Somme. Was the Somme begotten by the dark Christian chronicle? Christian nations, all of them.

Sherborne smelled of that chronicle. When he could, he turned west and south, towards Dorchester eventually. The colours came back shyly after the stormy night.

So fresh the ground, paths, hedges, the dripping trees. Grass washed perfectly green. Air motionless and satisfied. Nothing on the move but me. Chill tang of night still. I brought them all here, audience for my dice-show, now leave them asleep. But I cannot escape it. Suicide? I won't do that. Not with my own hand. Unthinkable. I'm not the one for that. Not cool enough, calculating, courageous. Am I a coward? Not back then, in the rough and tumble. Not on the rugby pitch. That's easy. Running, fighting, pitching in. It's the cold rehearsed stuff that's difficult. Time to change your mind. To weigh the odds. I talked my way into things and out of things. Riding on the back of words. Making people believe what I said. Making myself believe. Jack the gabber. Looks like a man. Talks clever. Emphatic and weighty. Deep voice. But he ran away.

I ran away. Only three words to say that, and no other will do. It was too much for me. I couldn't handle it. Couldn't go on. Couldn't pick up my mucky rifle again and clean it. Didn't trust the officers. Orders, rotas and fatigues and all the top-heavy sham of things. Couldn't think of a real thing to say anymore. Couldn't reach out and slap someone on the back. Didn't want to think of home. Didn't know what home was. Began wondering if the sky was real or whether I made it. I asked the dice. Is the sky real? Pillar Three, it said. The dolmen. Became so damn fast with the dice, knew them instantly. Pillar Three: roof of your curious grave, they said.

I'm through with the dice. Maggie never liked them. My darling Maggie. It was her who took them, I suppose. Sneaked them off the table while clearing up and then shouted at me after. Quite right. I needed shouting at. Got everyone mixed up in this running away and now I'm leaving again. Maggie came to me and I left her too. Had to. The priest was right about that. Should never have left the note for her. But if I hadn't, she wouldn't have … we wouldn't have. I'd never have known. I'd never have *known* her. Bible has good words. We knew each other.

Bibleblack path under the trees. Yielding so soft to the hoof. Lovely scuffing sound of the hoofs in the soil. Behind us a line of prints like cups. Is that what we leave, after? A line of cuplike prints. Here we drank, here feasted, here gave thanks. Will anyone ever see them to read? Jack's prints on the soft soil of the world. Jack the gadder.

I don't mind dying. I can stand there without moving in front of the wall. I can suffer the blindfolding, the commands. I can do that without crying out, breaking down. I'm almost sure of that. I will not break down or cry out. As for death, father did it. Millions have. The pain will come before. The cell. The dark walls again. Might madden me. Terrifying thought. Worse than death. Going mad in a cell. No sky even. No dice to ask. No rifle to clean. Then out into the theatre of their court. I won't answer their questions because they do not know what questions to ask. They will be uniforms, not people. I have seen them like that. Bobbing uniforms, caps, medals, all covered up. Did you or did you not …? I did and I would again. Remember that. *I did and I would again*. But you ran away. That's the very truth. For that they will shoot you, and rightly so.

Out of the woods now. Common land, starting to rise. Between banks of dry bracken like small soldiers shot with arms outstretched. The winter rains will beat them down, dull them and defeat them. Nothing eats bracken, not even bugs. Museum of summer stuff gone hard and brown. Useless even when green. Beautiful though, the first furl of growth, like a little fist raising. Even bracken has its moment, near the beginning. I had moments, near the beginning. With father over the fields. By the river on summer evenings. With mother, I suppose, but can't think of that now. Don't want to make her ashamed. Make her ashamed even though she's dead. Aye, there's the rub.

We live our lives seeking the approval of men. Fathers, brothers, teachers, sergeants. Bill Bate who fought me, Cockler who knows how to laugh, even though he shot an officer. But it's women that define us. If the teacher or the sergeant tells me well done, I'm happy for a   moment, but it's only for a moment. If my mother is ashamed of me, it's a life sentence. Maggie says to me she loves me, and I know it's for always. Beyond the grave. She tells me how she threw the handful of earth at the funeral, and the picture is alive forever because she is always present in what she says, all of her without exception or   reserve, just as when she saw the crumbs of soil sprinkle on the lid. But there's part of a man that's not quite there, as if he keeps it somewhere else. A kind of hiding or disappearing, not subtle or admirable in any way, but more like a forgetfulness, as if he can't quite remember where he left the rest. It's somewhere, but where exactly? Damned if I know.

Climbing. Eagerness of the horse to muscle upward. Feel it in his shoulders, flanks, and the power from behind. In his head thrusting forward. Even the ears have it, cocking and twitching. But his eyes don't change, if I could see them. In the blue-yonder eyes of a horse is the horse's amazement at the hugeness of the world it lives in, a world without borders or clocks. Once I looked into a horse's eye of midnight blue, and all I saw was a tiny picture of myself, right at the middle. Jack the lad.

It's not Dorchester I'm headed to. It's the Giant. Where else but the high Cerne wargod? Walked to the Giant with father once on Halloween. Took all morning, and when we got there we sat down and had a picnic in his right eye. Let's not mess with the sinister eye, Louis said. Picnic with father in the Giant's eye. Afterwards we built a fire which he started with a stick on a stone. Wildfire he called it. 'Wildfire for Samhain!' he shouted. There were moments, near the beginning.

Women pulling turnips in a sodden field. Looked up at me. What did they see? Big chap on a powerful horse. One called out something I couldn't hear. Made the others laugh. Keeping cheerful among the cold muddy roots. This ridge leads to the Giant. Trod it with Louis that time, felt to be above the whole world. Still feels like that. A little bump of upland and the world beneath falls away. Trains, towns and armies made to vanish by a ten-minute climb.

You wouldn't have run away, Louis, would you. You would have waited for them, and told them when they came, and spoken out at their trials and tribunals. You would have told it as it was, father mine. Tell you what, I'll build a fire for you here on the Trendle. Like the one we did together. Bigger even. Wasn't there for your funeral. Build a pyre and send a message wherever you are. Everything wet but no matter. Bracken for tinder! See, it does have its uses. Everything has its uses otherwise God wouldn't have bothered making it. What? Did God make everything? The cannons and the machine guns and the hell of the Somme? Bracken, okay. Trees, rivers, all that. But who invented the cannon? Men. Godless men. Are there such creatures? Maybe I'm one. No godless mouse is possible, so how godless men. Godless child? No. We lose God, that's what happens. We avoid him first, then we forget, then we deny He Ever Was. Then we invent the cannon. Big breach, big ball, maximum destruction. Gulliver knew that. Swift, I mean. Good King of Brobdingnag, appalled by the inventions of the West.

Crumbled bracken makes perfect tinder. Caught fire first time. Maybe they used it for the early muskets. Now for the big stuff. Bring it up from below. I want you to be proud, Louis, from up there ... My billows of smoke shall be seen in the heavens!

At ease now. Why? Climbing the hill, building the fire, hearing the flames crackle. Universal therapies for the collapsing soul: make fires on hilltops, stand guard over sandcastles threatened by the waves, make dams on brooks with stones and mud! Get out, climb up, make for the hills and the seas.

Know what I'll do now. The red die was wrong. Sword, it should have said. Pay the price, speak out. Write to Russell and the rest of them. Maybe Russell would come to the trial. If they let him. Not likely in the little world of the modern major-general. Little. It *is* little. Blew up half the continent of Europe but still a little, little world. Tum-tum-ta-ta, *he is the very model of a modern-major-general.* Tum-tum-ta-ta, Jack's the very model of deserting-frontline-corporals. Missed out the objecting bit. Jack's the very ... Jack's the very ... Can't do it. Try smoke signals with Charles's jacket instead. His tailored jacket, now in service for the making of Indian smoke message.

Not so easy, it appears. Leave the jacket too long it'll burn. On and off quick. But the smoke follows it. How to avoid? Like a matador's cape perhaps. Whisked on, whisked off. That's better. One billow rising up there. Look out, Louis, here it comes. Damn me, it's a good one. Still going up. But what does it say? It says: Peace! Rest in peace, Louis. Live in peace down there all you good folk. Learn, you warriors and kings, learn. Peace, my lovely Maggie Fox, with me or without me.

He watched his signal change its shape, growing broader and flatter, twisting about itself in the air above him. He watched two holes emerge in the smoke and a third larger hole below them, like a gash, and above it all an elongating wisp. It was the face he had seen in his dream on Bulbarrow. A face made of smoke with sockets for eyes and ridges for eyebrows, a valley for a mouth, hillocks where the cheekbones would be and the club held aloft. For what seemed a long while, this visage hung in the air above him, staring at him, and then the smoke began to dissolve like flesh dissolves after death, until at last all that was left was a skeleton of white growing slowly thinner.

Chapter Eleven

Day of the Dead

Some deny the antiquity of the Cerne Giant, calling it a medieval fertility symbol or a mischievous prank. No archaeological evidence, they say. What evidence do they expect from shallow cuts in chalk? No record in the old archives, they insist. There are explanations for that, never set down and later forgotten. The Giant hides the five signs of the old sorcerers, which together made their God of War. Prank? Fertility symbol? Would that it were!

(Louis Yeoman, *Journals*)

DURING the night, the thunderstorm had cracked on eastwards, and afterwards it had rained and rained, a steady downpour that soaked what was not already soaked and filled the brooks and ponds and water butts of middle Dorset, and washed the houses and barns and churches and sheds and found the leaks in the roofs, and flooded out families of mice and rats, driving them into winter quarters. Even the old house of *The Duntish Rings* got its fresh migration of rodents, to the deep pleasure of Toddy and Stout, champion ratters, who surprised a gang of young black rats in the feed bin the next morning. Sometime before dawn the rain had stopped, leaving the land drenched and violently laundered to the last twig and leaf.

First up after Jack left was Bill Bate, dejected but with sense of duty unimpaired, ready to stand before the squire and declare himself a murderer and take what came. Policemen, cells, judges. There was no reason why they wouldn't string him up. Murder was murder.

Yet he hesitated, wanting to tease out his last hours of freedom, before the curtain fell. He strolled in the vicinity of the inn, casting his eye over the way the buildings were made, admiring the stone arch-way that connected two of them. By the walled garden, he frowned at how the wall had been put up without a buttress. But there were rows of winter greens, and patches of garden herbs still: spearmint and lavender; parsley, sage, rosemary and thyme. His mother used to sing him that song and he missed her keenly. If he could have loved his wife as he loved his mother ... but it was a foolish thought.

A door in the far wall led to the edge of the woodland and a great oak grew hard by the wall, overshadowing a corner of the garden. A vigorous growth of ivy climbed up the trunk of this oak, and Bate got hold of it close to the ground and tore it away from the tree. He took out his knife and severed the stem and then for good measure hacked a second cut through the ivy by the ground. He found himself holding a twisted stem of ivy as thick as his wrist and he saw that it resembled the figure of a man sitting with crossed legs. When he had cleared away the leaves and tendrils, he found that this ivyman had a long face with mournful features, and that the thighs and calves of his legs were perfectly fashioned. He was about to toss it away into the bushes but checked, putting the figure in his rucksack instead.

There was a badger set further on, and beyond that rabbit holes, and the animals had been out early over the sodden land. The heavy dog-like prints of the badger and the little bunny paws in pairs. He came on the body of a half-grown rabbit and knelt by it to see how it had died. By the neck were two small holes as if drilled, so he searched further afield and found the weasel's prints, too, no bigger than weskit buttons.

178

He picked up the rabbit. A single bite at the back of the base of the neck. It was hardly big enough for the pot, hardly worth the skinning, but it might do for Cockler's dog, he thought.

The landlady was up, offering him eggs and bacon for breakfast. Cockler, stretched out by the fire, opened an eye and closed it again. Bate complimented Mrs Dooley on her winter greens and said he'd pulled up the ivy that was getting hold of the big oak beyond the garden. He showed her the ivyman and she took it at once although he had been thinking of showing it to his daughters when he got home, if he was allowed home. What an odd little body, she said and threw it on the fire before he had time to protest. Being wet as well as green, it sizzled and spat and contorted as the sap grew hot. Bate saw the long face of the ivyman rise from the fire and give an anguished look around the room before subsiding into the flames.

'An ivyman can kill an oak, William Bate, so perhaps we shouldn't wonder at him hopping in the heat,' Mrs Dooley said.

'Why so quick to throw it on the fire?'

'Because people can get to gazing on such curiosities, or propping them up where they've no business, or sticking pins in them for all I know, which isn't the right medicine for a little wooden doll. Help yourself to more bacon and I can cook another egg to go with it, if you like, since my hens are laying as if it were April.'

'Then yes I will, Mrs Dooley, and thank you for it.'

The smell of breakfast roused Cockler from his blanket, and they heard him whistling in the courtyard while performing his ablutions at the water barrel and calling out to his dog. He came back in with hair wet and drops of water running down his face, nose in the air to catch the whiff of bacon. Bate told him that there was a rabbit for the dog if he wanted it, hanging up in the stable.

'You're full of little gifts, this morning, William Bate,' Mrs Dooley commented, and Bate thought that there would be an end to such things when the hanging judge donned his cap.

He finished his breakfast and left. He decided against taking the horses. He couldn't abide the thought that the squire might take their safe return as a bribe, an inducement. An hour to Minterne? Maybe more in the wet. He went by the road to avoid the worst of the mud. So he missed seeing the line of cup-like prints made by Jack's horse over the soggy glebe.

The landlady of *The Duntish Rings* cleared the breakfast and prepared her account. Beef stew for five, ale and rum to order. Bedrooms, two, with fires. Half-a-dozen hen's eggs and half a pound of bacon. Stabling and grain for three horses. Six shillings in sum. Cockler found her writing up this document and offered to pay it with a half-sovereign. There was an outstanding account between himself and the captain, he explained, due to a misunderstanding at the time of their meeting. He insisted that Mrs Dooley take the ten shillings, and return the change to the captain when he reappeared.

'For myself, Missus, I've had two of the best meals that have come my way since leaving London town,' he said. 'The pleasure has been doubled by having these meals cooked and served up by a handsome woman like yourself. Being quick-witted as well as good to look at, you've no doubt cottoned on to what's afoot, which is certain so-called gentlemen keen to bring young John Yeoman to book for something there should be no law against. I knew you was sharp,

Missus, the moment I spotted you palming them dice that was causing Johnny to get so heated. I was on the point of doing it meself, but my way would've been to pick 'em up, open the door and throw 'em over the barn. Your way was neater. Without wishing it, I'd somehow caused this business, because it was the captain that was on 'is case and it was me that brought 'im 'ere. I would've taken 'im safely in the opposite direction if I'd known. I don't want ten shillings for causing that sort of bother; it'd burn a hole in my pocket. And now I'd best be off, Missus, for I've a long way to go.'

'There's business awaiting you, I'm sure, Mr Cockler.'

'I couldn't rightly say so, Mrs Dooley, but I'm hoping that I'll find something profitable to turn my hand to.'

'And what sort of thing might that be?'

'To tell you the truth, Mrs Dooley, there aren't many tools I haven't picked up, from a plough to a pipe wrench. You might think I'd find employment soon enough, but these is difficult times for the innocent as well as the guilty, if you get my meaning.'

'I do, Mr Cockler.'

'Now there's things I wouldn't want to tangle with, like any kind of doctoring or wordmongering, having a horror of blood and bile and being easily fatigued by what's written in books, but show me a device made of timber or iron, Mrs Dooley, and I'll fix it so it works.'

'My house has good water, Mr Cockler, from a deep well, but it's a little way off from the house and it's a labour to fill the basins and jugs every day, especially if I have other tasks.'

'I'll readily see to your jugs for you, Mrs Dooley, before I go. Just say the word.'

'It's not what I had in mind. They tell me a mechanical pump and some pipes would bring the water directly to the house, provided the water level's high enough.'

'That much would be easy, Missus, and then all you'd need is to get some power to your pump and put a tank in your loft and you could have a tap in your kitchen and one in your washroom too.'

'What power?'

'Wind power, animal power, something simple. You wouldn't need for your pump to work more than half-an-hour a day to top the tank up.'

'Could you build me such a system, Mr Cockler?'

'I could, Mrs D, with a decent pump and some lengths of pipe and a few other bits and pieces.'

'These would be available in one of the local towns, I take it.'

'They would, Missus.'

'Then if your other plans allow it, Mr Cockler, I would employ you here at five shillings a week plus bed and board for as long as the job took.'

So it was arranged between them and when Cockler stepped out to see to his horse and skin the rabbit and settle his wagon for a longish halt, he wondered what he had done to earn a billet in a public house run by a good-looking widow. 'Yer luck's turning, Cockler old cock,' he said to himself.

Marguerita Dooley looked forward to running water in her house, but there were the moods to reckon with too. Cockler's humour was a keen blade, and there should be a sword for All Hallows. She patted the pocket of her apron where the dice were. 'Not just his bonny hair and his fiddler's fingers,' she murmured to herself as she made her way to the barn. And again she felt the pocket of her apron to make sure that the dice were still where she had put them the night before.

By the feed bin she found the bodies of two dead rats, which she picked up by their tails. Stepping outside, she flung them over the hedge into the woods. She looked behind the bin to see if her cats had left any other of their victims about, and there in a nest of hay lay a large black tomcat which looked fiercely at her through one eye. The other eye was swollen and closed, with a gash over it that had bled and matted the hair. The hackles rose on the cat's neck and its mouth opened in a faint yowl of warning.

'Now then, pussy,' she said. 'I'll have none of your incivility in my own place, thank you.' But if the behaviour of the tomcat was incivil, that of Marguerita Dooley was ruthless. Even as she spoke she was feeling behind her for the six-pronged pitchfork standing by the bin and in a swift and decisive movement she raised it high in both hands and drove it at the creature's body. But the tomcat was quicker, twisting away from the points of the fork as they were almost on him and uttering a squeal of rage as the outermost prong nicked the flesh of his hind leg.

The fork buried itself in the wadge of hay. As Marguerita struggled to pull it free, she was hit by a powerful blow on the back of her head and fell forward onto the hay, stunned. When she sat up and looked round, the creature was gone from the barn. Dimly she remembered the sound of its heavy scampered steps.

She kept the pitchfork with her as she went out. It was by her side as she searched the muddy yard for signs. But Jack had been through with his horse, and Cockler for his wash and Cockler's dog had been about and Bate had strolled to and fro, so there was nothing to be learned. She circled the buildings of the inn looking for footprints or a window broken open, and then she went to the barn, carrying the pitchfork with her. In the barn, she found Cockler sitting on the straw by a pile of his stuff, with his dog next to him, asleep.

'What ho, Mrs D! I hope it's not me you're looking for, armed like that,' Cockler said.

'Please search the buildings for an intruder, Mr Cockler.'

He was on his feet at once. 'Of what sort?' he said.

'A dangerous sort. Didn't your dog hear anything?'

'There was a black-and-white collie about earlier, Mrs D. My old feller had gone to see 'im off, I reckon.'

Marguerita hastened across the yard to the inn and went inside. She looked for mud on the floor, on the stair, but there was none. Upstairs, the doors of the bedrooms were shut. She knocked quietly at the first room and went in to rouse Margaret Fox.

Maggie came to with a puzzled look.

'Your man went off early on the piebald,' Marguerita said. 'If you want to go after him, you'd best go now while the captain's still asleep. In my store, there was a black tomcat with a bad eye. Not one of mine. I gave him a scare but he's around still is what I think. Mr Cockler's looking out for him.'

'For the cat.'

'I can ask him to get your horse ready,' Marguerita said. 'There's an old saddle and bridle that might do. I won't be wanting them back and you'll get on quicker and safer with a saddle.'

'I'll take both horses.'

'But you'll let me keep the dice for a while, m'dear.'

Maggie shook her head. 'I'll need them,' she said, holding out her hand.

'There's a reason for me to look after them now,' Marguerita said.

'They're mine, you said, and I should have them.'

The older woman drew them from the pocket of her apron and passed them over, reluctantly.

While Maggie was dressing, she heard Sylph call shrilly from the barn. The filly didn't like being saddled, she thought. When she got downstairs, she found that it wasn't that. The bay mare was gone from the stable and Sylph was calling out for her friend.

Cockler's search for the intruder had extended to the garden, the sheds and the edge of the woods.

''E must 'ave took the horse while I was in the woods. The gun we brought over from Hammond 'as gone missing too,' he said. 'The dog was with me and you was still inside, I suppose, Mrs D. But he must 'ave been sharp about it. I wasn't gone more than a few minutes. And where the hell was he hid while I was in and out of the buildings? And who was 'e, anyway?'

'Don't mind that for the moment, Mr Cockler. Margaret knows who he was, I expect.'

The girl nodded. 'I know who he was, and I know where he's gone, and I must be there before him,' she said.

'You've got the right little horse for it on ground like this,' Cockler said.

Mrs Dooley tied Maggie's satchel to the pommel of the saddle. 'I packed some apples and a slice of bread and cheese,' she said. 'You'll come back and see me when it's all done, Margaret Fox?'

'I will,' she said.

She rode out of the gateway and up the lane.

Not long after she was gone, Charles clumped downstairs demanding to know where his brother was and why the bedroom was locked.

'Your brother left at dawn, Captain Yeoman, and it's my habit to keep the bedrooms locked when they're unoccupied,' said Mrs Dooley. She offered him eggs and bacon.

The captain had no time for breakfast. He shot out a volley of questions, which Cockler casually batted back. Please wake Margaret, the captain told Mrs Dooley, but she answered that the girl too had ridden off and no, she had no idea where to.

'Mentioned something about yer father's place,' Cockler said.

'That's where Jack will be as well,' Charles muttered. 'Cockler, I'll need your help with the motorcycle.'

They went out together and Cockler gestured the captain out of the way while he lifted out the machine.

'I'll see about the dead man while I'm in Hammond,' Charles said as he mounted the Zenith. 'If my brother's there, he'll be on his way to Dover by midday. If anyone comes asking, you can tell them that.' The captain fired up the motorbike and swept out of the yard into the road.

Charles Yeoman found no one at his father's cottage and no corpse in the porch. His enquiries among the neighbours discovered only that there had been some people at the cottage the afternoon before who'd left on horseback before the rain set in. Being Sunday, the village store was closed and Hammond had no inn. Charles had a slight acquaintance with one of the Hammond farmers, but this man knew nothing of any accident. It occurred to Charles that his brother had cooked up this story with Bate in order to … in order to do what, though?

He went to find Grammer Score, who had brought Louis milk and cheese and cooked for him on occasion and who had discovered him dead. Grammer lived with her sister at the end of a narrow lane running between deep banks of holly that led only to the one cottage. The thatch came down so low as to scratch the heads of visitors when they went in and there was more straw than clay in the old bending walls. The cow lived at one end of the cottage, the better end some would say, and the two old women at the other.

'Were that you fiddlin' about at yer father's place yestereen?' Grammer Score said. It was his brother Jack, Charles said. 'I thought that one were at war,' said Grammer.

'He came home, Grammer.'

'Thank the lord fer that,' the old lady muttered. 'If 'er came round to see 'er father's place, why didn'er call on Grammer to open up for 'er? I would've done it and gladly. I'd 'ave showed 'er what there was to show and told 'er what there was to tell. Bain't right going in on a place empty when the dead 'ave scarce left it. The dead don't go far for the first forty day as yer well know yerself.'

'I don't subscribe … '

'Bain't no *subscription* necessary. 'Tis a fact that the dead stay among us for the first forty days, that's what. 'Tis in the bible, and

187

even if it weren't, there's plenty of folk that 'ear 'em about doing the same stuff they was doing for years before. My own mother would hear father going out to wash every morning whistling as 'er always did, and she swore that the whistling stopped on the fortieth day exact. She got out the calendar and reckoned it out. Forty days exact. So don't you go telling me that there isn't something left of a fine man like Louis Yeoman, a larger man than yerself and yer brother put together, a month to the day after he passed over. Come on,' she said, 'you'd best pay a visit.'

She refused to climb on the motorbike, so he drove back to Louis's cottage and waited for her impatiently, not going in until she arrived. She came with the front door key and unlocked for him and herded him in as if he might run away.

'There's somebody been reading 'is books,' she said, looking round. 'Yer brother I suppose, although why 'er couldn't put them back where they belong I don't know. I'll step outside and sit on the bench in the garden, and you can take a while with yer father on yer own. I'll be there if you need me.'

'Grammer, I heard tell of a fight here yesterday, and a man killed. Did you get wind of such a thing?'

'Did I get wind, 'er asks? Last time I got wind was when the 'taters 'ad the blight and the wheat were mouldy and all we 'ad to eat for a month o' Sundays were dry beans.'

'I meant ... '

'I know what you meant Charles Yeoman. There weren't no fight 'ere yesterday that I heard of.'

'It was my own brother told me, Grammer. There was a dead man in the porch here, he said.'

'Did 'er so? Well there bain't one now. But then t'was the eve of All Hallows and there's no tellin' what goes on when the spirits are abroad. Like as not, yer brother got a sight of summat he didn't ought of. When yer father were 'ere, lord rest 'im, Grammer saw to the garlic 'n that and made certain there was a proper fire going, but yer brother wouldn't think o' such business now would 'er.'

Charles went into his father's house and was alone there for the first time. He found himself going on tiptoes up the stairs as if he might disturb something and felt the enormous absence in the tiny bedroom with its bed neatly made and a book on the bedside table, which was *Dombey and Son.* There was nothing so rich and strange as old Dickens, Louis used to say, nothing better for winter nights, and Charles had a sudden vision of those long nights here in the quiet cottage with no sons and no sound at all, just the old man reading Dombey by the lamp upstairs. Why were so many of these long tales about fathers who fought with sons and fathers who lost sons and sons who lost fathers without understanding what they had lost? Then he remembered that *Dombey and Son* was really about a father and daughter, which made him think of Maggie Fox who maybe loved Louis more than either of them. More than me certainly, he thought. I don't love much. Why? There's no lack of feeling in my heart, but I must keep it turned down. Well of course I must, you can't have it bursting out all over the shop, can you. It'd get in the way of … of everything. How would you work, make decisions, act when you need. How could I have run the farm if I'd let the pages of my heart open where they would?

But they'd fallen open now, and the house felt very still and too large and the well of sorrow very deep, so he tiptoed downstairs and sat down in his father's chair to get steady again. He picked up the journal that the priest had been reading the day before and that too fell open, according to the rule of forty days or according to some other rule, at the following passage:

Charles doesn't visit because he is ashamed of my living pauperlike in this distant spot, and Jack can't visit, Lord save him and keep him, and Maggie comes when she can, bless her heart. Charles thinks of me as an old wastrel, I suppose, or maybe he's hurt that I didn't stay on at Manston, even though he got on better there without me. All this supposing! We spend long years together but we don't know each other, because we hardly know our own selves. Honestly and bluntly, we don't. Charles thinks he is dull and unimaginative next to Jack but this is so in the very narrow sense that Charles does not act on impulse. He does not realise that his courage and determination set the rest of us free.

Charles closed the journal. He had to find Jack. Get him on a coach back to France. But where the devil had he gone since he was not here in Hammond? Somewhere on a hilltop, looking out, or by a stream, looking in. Or on the train to Bristol or London. 'Bluntly and honestly, I have no idea,' he thought. He said goodbye to Grammer Score in the garden of the cottage and fired up the Zenith to drive back to Duntish.

Chapter Twelve

Listen, Sylph

'Orses and dorgs is some men's fancy. They're wittles and drink to me.

(Charles Dickens)

IN the space of forty-eight hours, Maggie Fox had been lost in a fog, poisoned by a priest, and knocked unconscious in a fall from her horse. She had witnessed a man die a violent death, been attacked by a maddened cat and lain with her lover, a deserter, for the first time. She had discovered that she was the youngest member of an ancient order of … of witches, and the owner of two numinous dice that people might kill for.

She was tough. If she had not been, she would have been overwhelmed by three strong men, even though they loved her. She could walk ten miles and ride twenty. At the harvesting of the potatoes and the bailing of the hay, she worked as long and hard as the men. She stood up for herself in an argument and her tongue – when she was roused – was no doubt the sharpest in the family. If anybody said, or implied, that she was 'just a girl', her eyes flashed and a retort leapt to her lips. She was tough and she was proud, but now she was shaken. The thornapple ride had wobbled her world and it would not stay still.

She knew where she had to go, even if she did not understand how she knew. It had come to her the night before, in the instant when sleep had arrived but did not yet rule, an instant big as a world, fleeing as it came. She had seen the signs of the Giant lit by fire at night and the mystery of the dice was made plain. Put into words, it shrunk and

191

dimmed, impaled on the barbs of time. The sword was the power of the Giant, the pillar its emblem, the tower its form, the skull was its mind and the circle was its wheel where men and dice spun and spun. The Margarets' cross was shining on the abbey in the valley below. It was to the Giant that Maggie was bound.

On their way were swollen streams, paths turned to mud, the fear of coming upon the priest unawares. But there were quiet times too, plodding over the sodden tilth or following an easy path under trees, and there were deep matters to unravel. She needed to talk to somebody, and there was only Sylph. She spoke out loud, although from time to time the words turned inward, as a stream disappears underground.

'You see, Sylph,' she said. 'There was *nothing there* as the cat ran to the door. If I had seen it go from the room, then yes, maybe it was just a cat all along and I was spooked, as Marguerita said. But she said it to comfort me. Otherwise, why all those warnings about how he could change his shape and come in without using the door? And why doesn't he fly to the Giant, then, as a sorcerer would? Isn't that what sorcerers do, Sylph? If a man can take the shape of a cat, then why not the shape of … an eagle, say, which could be at the Giant in ten minutes, swoop down and take what it has come for?

'What I believe is that he was somewhere close by, *muddling my mind.* It's obvious that people can do that sort of thing, especially when you've been made to drink a kind of poison that changes the texture of things. Three days, she said, and this is the third day. It's with me still, like a shadow on a sunless morning. I was muddled and scared and it made me vulnerable.

'It wasn't a dream. Not like you and I know dreams. Do you dream, I wonder, Sylph, when you close your eyes? You do, I'm sure. You dream of lush meadows, and of open plains where you can gallop without stopping, or maybe of being chased by a pack of wild dogs. You don't like dogs, I know.

'There were voices from elsewhere that night on the marsh. It isn't the voices that bother me so much, but what I want to know is *where is the elsewhere*? It seemed to me like another planet of thought going on all the time beyond our reach, higher or deeper, but still real. That's the point. What I think is that the priest of evil – it's how he described himself – has a way of getting to me in that other realm. *Realm* was the word she used. The realm of the dice, obeying a different law. *He* exists in the realm of the dice is what I think. But Jack doesn't, obviously, even though he's been carrying those little cubes around with him for months and rolling them out at the drop of a hat. Marguerita's got a foot in both camps, and perhaps I have too, now that the dice are mine, whatever that may mean.'

They were following the course of a big ditch bordering a meadow. As they approached the corner of the field, a pond came into view, fringed with reeds.

'What it means is that I could fling them in that pond. Look, it's very deep. Hardly more than the spot where the ditches meet, but it's got that look about it. A blueish glow just beneath the surface of the water. If I throw them in there, they won't be found for a hundred years, or ever. Charles would do it, in an instant, and Cockler probably. But it was she that gave them to me, and I believe in her. I liked her from the first.

'I can tell you something, Sylph, and really I couldn't tell it to anyone else. Even to Louis if he were alive. Not to Jack, for sure, because he'd think of it as some kind of girlish thing. Imagine. You're an eighteen-year-old girl and you haven't done anything much – well, nothing beyond the home and the farm. You haven't painted a beautiful picture or planted a wonderful garden or had some grand person fall in love with you or even caught a huge fish. You've known only ordinary things, an ordinary life.

'You're an ordinary sort of girl called Margaret and here comes someone older, and wiser. Yes, really *wiser*. You can see it in her eyes, in her hands even, in the way she carries herself. What was it she said? "I let them think that Dooley was my man." That's extraordinary, if you think about it. She's an extraordinary woman, running that place by herself, sleeping there alone, with the rings forming nightly in her fire. Making medicines for sick people, in return for a basket of sticks or a handful of fruit. And when she meets me, she says to me almost at once, you're a *Margaret*, and this name I've had since I was born suddenly has a different feel to it, as if it were very special. She tells me that I'm part of something that connects me to a long and dangerous history, something much bigger and older than myself, older than churches. There was a woman, she said, Peg or Meg, who was burned for what she painted on her fireplace. *What could it have been that she painted there?* Not roses and forget-me-nots. What do people get burned for? For something to which they are sworn, or for some practice they will not put away. Women of my stripe, she said, and I felt I would be proud to be a woman of her stripe. You see what I mean, Sylph? You see why I couldn't fling the dice into the pond? Because of her. And because of Louis, who gave them to Jack before he went to war. Louis knew, she said. His last gift to his son: two dice, one red, one white.

'What I'm going to do is to give them to the priest. She must have guessed what was on my mind – divined it, she might say – because she didn't want me to take the dice with me. Last night she was urging me to take them and this morning she wants to keep hold of them. But listen, Sylph, what I think is that the priest cannot do anything with these dice. Whatever is their power it will be inaccessible to him. I saw him that night of the thornapple ride. I saw *through* him. I saw his slinking, filching ways. I saw the meanness and the hardness of him. If there was anything large, or generous, or humorous in him, he would be a man to fear. Don't you think, Sylph, that all those villains of history, Napoleon and Genghis Khan, don't you think that there must have been in their character something grand, something brave or magnanimous? Otherwise, history would have passed them by. What about Judas Iscariot, you'll say, but after he had done what he did, he returned the thirty pieces of silver and he hanged himself. I think only a brave man can hang himself.

'There is nothing in the so-called priest except what is selfish and envious. He prepared a poison for me to drink when I'd hardly sat down in his house. Two travellers arrive in the fog and he brings them into his house and gives them a drink to knock them senseless. Poisoned tea and Urley gin. He didn't know about the dice then. He didn't know about the desertion. Why did he do it? There couldn't have been any *logical* reason for it. It was something like an experiment. Of course, I'm only a woman, and to him all women are to be despised, that's obvious. If he hadn't despised me, he might have attacked me that night, in my bedroom. It would have been a matter of indifference to him. You know what I think, Sylph? If I give him the dice, they will *destroy* him! Ruin him or drive him mad.

'Marguerita must know more than me about these things, you're thinking. But maybe not. She doesn't like the dice and they don't like her, she said. She doesn't want to use them, even in healing. Perhaps already I understand them better than she.'

They went through a gateway onto a road. The horse went to follow the road uphill, but Maggie reined her in.

'Hold on, Sylph. We cross the road here and head for Buckland by the footpath. I know where we are. I've walked here with Louis.'

But Sylph refused to go on even when prodded.

'You're taking me to Minterne, aren't you? You want to go *home*. Alright then, that's the way we'll go. We've got speed on our side, so we'd better use it. Take me to Minterne, Sylph! Then along the highway to Cerne at a gallop. The priest will keep to the fields. He's on the squire's horse and he'll keep out of sight. But even on his own horse, he'd choose the hidden ways. It's his nature. We'll go by the roads, and we won't even see him.'

They rode up the road, the girl watching the village of Buckland grow smaller over her shoulder.

'How can I know more of the dice than Marguerita, when they've only been mine for a night and a day?' she said after a while. 'But she gave them to me not as a gift but because they belonged to me. They had always been mine, she meant. Then why did Louis give them to Jack, if he *knew*? Think of that evening. He wanted to give Jack something precious because he was going to war and might never return. He must have felt that they had some protective power, like a charm or amulet. Charles told me once that lots of the men in the trenches had their lucky mascots, a lock of someone's hair, their mother's old prayer book, a lucky coin. They believed in them, he said. Some of them would panic if they mislaid them and had to go into battle without them.

'Perhaps Louis hoped that since the dice were due to come to me, they were a kind of guarantee that Jack would return. He didn't know that they'd become an addiction. Not even Louis could have imagined what the trenches were like, I suppose. But you know, Jack never said that it was the dice that told him to walk away from the war. He never asked them about that, I'm sure. He used them like a person tossing a coin. Probably a coin would have done him just as well. Most of the time, he was just asking them, shall I do this, or that? Heads or tails? And then he did what he was going to do in the first place. "Skull One? We'll take the horses." Why, for goodness' sake? Surely Skull One would mean, look out, don't take those horses. If we hadn't taken the horses, we wouldn't have arrived at the marsh. Bate wouldn't have come after us. We would have gone quietly to Louis's cottage and thought things out.

'But Jack was right about one thing. The dice are thrown once. Complete the sentence, Marguerita kept saying, but that's not how they work! It might have been different for some careful healer long ago, trying to get to the root of a difficult illness. Maybe she needed to throw six times to determine the history of the illness, its likely course. Maybe that's where the *sentence* came in. But two dice thrown once give you thirty-six options. How many more do you need? How could you possibly *manage* two-hundred-and-sixteen options? The number of plants in the Dorset woods, she said, but you aren't going to choose between *all* of them, are you? If you're wondering whether mallow or nettle is the right medicine, you don't have to bother about deadly nightshade, do you?

'You throw the dice once, Sylph, and they tell you what's going to happen, if you're sharp enough to read them. Do I mean sharp? It's more than sharpness. Circle Six said the dice in the porch at Hammond, and it meant that we were going to *The Duntish Rings*, where there are six rings on the inn sign and six barrels in the taproom. But we couldn't have read that, could we? We didn't even know there was such a place. Maybe Bate did, but he wasn't interested in the dice. I watched him last night when Jack was making his throw in front of all of us, and I could see that he treated it as some kind of charade, or a piece of madness brought back from the war.

'Louis gave the dice to Jack. Marguerita gave them to me. I'm giving them to the priest. If I don't, he will take them, one night or another. I will make a bargain with him, he can have the dice and we will be rid of him.

'We must be rid of him, Sylph. I'm sure you can see that. As long as he's around, we can't get on with what really matters. Besides, I have thrown the dice only once and I threw the Skull One. I'd be a fool to ignore that, don't you think? Margaret or not. The Skull One points at the priest. I will give him the dice and they will destroy him.'

She said these words with a sudden intensity, and the pony jerked her head up and cocked her ears, as if there was danger about.

'I startled you, Sylph,' said the girl. 'But I must save Jack, you understand. He will not save himself. He will not hide and he will not keep quiet. So I have to save him and there is only one way for me to do it. I will convince him to return to his regiment in France. Yes, that comes as a surprise to you. But if he does not go back, he will get himself shot. Besides, he cannot bear it that he ran away. He hates the war, but underneath he wishes he hadn't left. If Long Rob had lived, or Long John or whoever it was, he probably wouldn't have. He's back here now, so what can he do but go on fighting? He's brave enough, but he won't work things out and make a plan. He'll just plunge in, as always. If he thinks about it for a moment, he'll see that he can do no good at all by speaking out against anything. He's a deserter! They won't give him a chance to open his mouth. They won't even let him make a speech to the firing squad. If he stays here, he'll be arrested today, or tomorrow, and they'll silence him, at once and forever. So he has to go back, and after last night, he will listen to me. Everyone thinks of Jack as a boisterous, combative sort of person. You wouldn't believe how gentle he can be. I wouldn't have believed it myself. Well, let that be. Let that be, Sylph. It doesn't belong to the realm of the dice. It has its own realm, with another name. Because he loves me, he'll go back to France. After the war he can fight those other battles in whatever way he can. After the war.

'After the war, I can get the dice back, if I have the courage. Perhaps Marguerita will help me. One day when the priest's away, with his horrid dog. Did the dog save my life that night in the fog? I might have lain there all night and been found dead in the morning. I shouldn't call him horrid, I suppose. Dogs aren't horrid unless their masters are. Marguerita recognised the dog by its flash. Does it matter, I said. Regrettably it does, child, she said.

'There's a jitteriness in me that I never felt before. They say that after an earthquake, people go about not trusting the earth to stay still under their feet. It's a bit like that, Sylph. But there's something else as well. Like when we arrived at that pond. It seemed to me that it came there like a vision, just at that moment when I was wondering about what to do with the dice. Suddenly, in a place where you'd think there would be no more than a puddle, there was this very old, very deep, blueish pool. There was the unmistakable feeling of great age. It's as if an ancient quality of things has become apparent to me. A profundity that has to do with time.

'Once I was woken from a dream by the back door banging. I know it was the back door that woke me because I heard Charles cursing it. The latch was worn and a strong wind would blow the door open and bang it shut again. Then I remembered my dream. I'd been running through a huge, dark house, in and out of the rooms, down the stairs and through the cellars, chasing somebody. Chasing myself, I think, odd though it may sound. The person I was chasing had no clothes on. Then I was running along a corridor and there was a light coming from the room at the end and I was running to reach the light, and just as I got there the door slammed in my face and I woke up. You see what I'm on about, don't you? It wasn't the banging of the front door which intruded into the dream as it were, because I was already dashing along a corridor towards an open door, and you might even say that the whole dream was leading up to that moment. If I could put this in the right words, you'd understand me, Sylph, because horses aren't stuck with the idea of time clicking along in a straight line like we are. There is an eternity of now in a horse's life. You know what I mean, girl, don't you?'

'I saw something last night, Sylph,' she said, 'just as I was dropping off to sleep. There's that moment, isn't there, between waking and sleeping? It's an instant that goes so quick that it ought not be able to contain anything at all. There's no space there, you would think, for a single thought. Yet just once or twice, that tiny gap in things is filled with a huge idea that you've never thought of before and which comes to you making perfect sense. As soon as it's come, it's gone, because either you fall asleep or you wake up and catch it but it slips away from you and leaves you clutching at nothing. Once in that instant there was a crowd on a lawn and a king in a glass-house in the middle of the lawn, and the crowd were praising their king but he was a man who knew nothing at all about anything. I caught this scene as it was breaking up and put it back together in my mind and it was a message, and the message was that the ignorance of the king was a reflection of the ignorance of his people. He was in a house made of glass where he could never hide and which would break into a thousand pieces if they started throwing stones. The price of kingship, I suppose. What was so odd and wonderful was that no part of it had been thought by me. It had come to me like a vision through that gap between the worlds. Maybe I'm peculiar. Maybe other people don't get such things.

'Last night it was the Giant I saw. I had a feeling already about the Giant. Perhaps I got it from the priest. He knew that whatever it was we were all caught up in would end there. "You and I have an appointment, long foretold," he said. I thought afterwards, as we were walking through the rain, that they must have been the last words he would ever speak. I was wrong about that. Now I'm keeping the appointment.

Chapter Thirteen

Warlord

The call of our country is the call of God. (Church Sermon, 1916)

CLIVE LAWRENCE ate an early breakfast in the Manor House at Minterne, sitting with his back to the glowing heat of the kitchen range, attended only by his housekeeper, who set his place and boiled his egg and brought more toast, butter and marmalade as necessary. The informality of this arrangement suited the squire's modest habits, because although a man of wealth and power by the standards of the neighbourhood, he had no love of extravagance and kept a household considered by other gentlemen as small to the point of impoverishment.

Both his parents had died when he was young and he had inherited a large tract of land containing valleys with rich soils and hillsides with good grazing and woodlands with tall timber, which some said made up the prettiest land in middle Dorset. He married the second of three daughters of Sherborne town but this marriage did not work out for either of them. He was young, handsome and rich, and what is more he was observant and astute, except where his wife was concerned. He did not notice the fine sensitivity of her intellect and could not account for the eccentricity of her needs, which made him at first impatient and ultimately neglectful. She grew ill and pale and would eat almost nothing for weeks at a time, becoming ethereally beautiful in the process. Everything would change if she had a child, Clive Lawrence thought, but when she did become pregnant, it killed her.

Clive Lawrence permitted himself no display of grief and none but himself can tell how much he felt. His housekeeper knew him better than most and said that it was the loss of the child and not of the woman that hurt him, and certainly it was children he wanted from his marriage not companionship, at least not after he realised that she could not come to him without him also coming to her. He saw no reason to change his habits, for he felt privately that the harmonies of his land and his Tudor mansion were a reflection of his desserts as a human being. His presumption of personal excellence had no element of boastfulness, because he never compared himself to others. The only person in his life really to suffer at his hands was his young wife, because she was the only person who came close enough to do so. When she died, he decided not to re-marry because why should he again risk such a disturbance to his equanimity? The death of the unborn child had killed in him any dreams of the dynastic kind. His acres would be left to his sister's sons, whom he scarcely knew.

When war was declared on Germany and Austria-Hungary, Clive Lawrence accepted it as a consequence of the natural scheme of things, which required Russia to dominate the Balkans and the Black Sea, the Ottoman Empire to be dissolved, with Egypt and the Levant and Mesopotamia falling to the British, and France to keep an eye on Germany. Italy could be left to squabble with Austria for the Tyrol and the Dalmatian coast and Britain would continue to rule the waves elsewhere at all points to India and beyond. Africa outside Egypt Lawrence considered a useless expanse which could be allowed to the French and to the minor Europeans. America would rule the Pacific, of course, and the one question mark in Lawrence's mind hung over

China. This was by no means a useless expanse and, together with its southern appendices – Burma, Siam and Cochin China – constituted the necessary extension of British rule in India. There might here be some conflict of interest with the United States, and for this reason the United States navy should never be permitted to become as powerful as the British. The United States could be allowed a free hand in Latin America, and might also be encouraged to take Japan. Australia would remain British since no one else could conceivably want it, being a kind of Africa of the South Seas.

Clive Lawrence deliberated these strategies in much the same way as he did the distribution of wheat, barley, pasture and vegetable crops over his own acres. In his study, he kept an 1895 edition of the *Times Atlas*, which had on its first page a map of the moon, giving its diameter as 2,162 English miles, but which was more often open on page 85, the map of China. He had a plan, as yet only dimly conceived, that when the war was over, he would travel to Hong Kong or Shanghai and purchase an interest in a trading company. His father had left him with bonds and deeds which might be converted into cash, and Clive Lawrence's private ambitions, particularly since the death of his wife, far exceeded the bounds of his Minterne estate. He had considered standing for Parliament, but lacked the connections and also any liking for speechifying and vote-getting. He preferred to act on his own and he saw China as the great unexploited opportunity. He read all he could get his hands on about the networks of the great commercial banks and trading companies of the east. He knew the whereabouts of Shantung and Chungking and Nanking. He was considerably interested in the prospects for Port Arthur and Fuchow

should Shanghai and Hong Kong prove too crowded with entre-
preneurs. Much of China was currently in the hands of the warlords,
he learned. He liked this word 'warlord'. There was something grand
and untrammelled in it. In his more extravagant moments, he saw
himself as a kind of warlord of middle Dorset. Occasionally he would
wear his father's sword when riding around his estate.

He acquired *The Chinese Language and How to Learn It* – 'intended
for the use of army officers and missionaries' – and learned that in
order to say 'Is his business a large one?' he had first to translate this
into 'His buy-sell large not large?' before looking up the necessary
ko's and *ta's* and *mai's* with which the sentence was constructed. It
was, he saw, not just a question of a different language but of a
different system of thought, one that was direct and simple but capable
of real subtlety, which matched his private assessment of his own
mind.

What concerned him that morning as he tackled his soft-boiled egg
was the matter of his missing horses and Captain Yeoman's brother.
He was angry about the horses, especially about the younger one, who
was well-bred and skittish and might do herself an injury. Besides, if
the animals fell into the hands of gypsies or pedlars, they could be out
of the county in no time and sold off who knows where. He had
disliked Captain Yeoman, whose deadline for the return of the horses
had anyway expired. Bill Bate had not reported back, and that was a
mystery, because Bill Bate was normally as dependable as one of his
own corner-stones. There had been no communication from the police.
By mid-afternoon of the day before, nowhere in the great web of his
estate had there been the quiver of an insect trying to make its escape.

There were foresters in the forests, and hedgers on the hedges and shepherds out with their sheep and on the roads were carters and marketers, but there had been no news of the horses or of the deserter.

The squire had instructed his bailiff to ride out round and ask for news, which took the bailiff as far as Middlemarsh and Buckland and involved him in how-d'ye-do's with tenants and tenants of tenants and even with ploughboys and priests. It was late in the afternoon before there was a whisper of what he sought. A man who had been hedging on the road by Hammond told the bailiff what he'd heard. A man had died in the village, so the story went, and the name of the killer was Bill Bate, and his companion was a deserter from the army. The bailiff was sure that Bill Bate was no killer, but the rain was pelting down by then and he was keen to get home.

Clive Lawrence had these scraps of information to toy with at his early breakfast: a sighting at Hammond in the afternoon and the odd fact that Bate was now apparently accompanying the man he had set out to bring to justice. As for the story of the killing, Lawrence discounted it as exaggeration or hearsay. If there had been a fight, it would have been between Bate and the deserter, he thought, and from this a false rumour had gone abroad.

He had his housekeeper fetch the bailiff, whom he sent for the chief whip of the Middle Dorset Hunt, even if it meant getting him out of bed. He met them at the kennels and told them to ready the dogs.

'I want a show, today, Bailie,' he said, 'because where there's a show there's rumour, and rumour travels fast. A fox can dig itself in, but a deserting soldier must hide among men, so it's among men that we'll be seeking.'

The squire knew that the passage of the hunt through the villages of middle Dorset, an event unknown during more than two years of war, would be a sure way of drawing the people and making the tongues wag. He drove his trap back to the manor, called in at the stables for them to put a saddle on his hunter, Firefly, found Clem Rose at the milking and told him what was up, then went into the house to change.

No red jacket today. Colonel's uniform of the Mid-Dorset Militia, smart as the real thing. Black line down the outside leg. Made one seem taller, straighter. Belt and spats stiff with blanco. Brass buttons and buckles gleaming, the lustre of the martial. Knew what they were doing, these army types. Who designed officer's uniforms? Collective wisdom of the military? Used to be reds and whites, showy. More practical now, solemn khaki, with the Sam Browne, a touch of the buccaneer. Who was Sam Browne? American Civil War, most likely. There was nothing quite like heroism in war. Not among pioneer airmen, inventors, engineers – not Brunel with his tunnels and bridges or politicians such as Palmerston and Peel. Peel had offended the landed interest. Burned in effigy, so they said. The real thing was war. Wellington, the iron duke. Marlborough, another duke. Were they all dukes? The grand old Duke of York. General Gordon, he was no duke. Chinese Gordon, fought whom in China exactly? Dissident warlords. What, all of them? Then died in the Sudan. Bible fanatic. Madman, some said, but still glorious, glorified.

Now for father's sword. Blooded in the Afghan wars. And lastly, the peaked cap of the colonel. What does the mirror say? Salute! Salute myself in the mirror. Glad Mrs Whosit didn't see that. *Saluting myself in the mirror!*

They gathered at the kennels, a handful of horsemen, some lads on foot, a score of yapping hounds. More than enough to cut a dash, Clive Lawrence thought. As they were getting ready to start, two men walked into the yard. The first was Christian Thick, with his axe over his shoulder. 'I came across Christian on the road,' Clem Rose said. 'I thought it'd be as well for him to be along with us. He can follow a set of prints from here to kingdom come.'

The second man was Bill Bate.

'Ah, Bate!' said Clive Lawrence. 'Where did you spring from? There's a story going around about you.'

'A word in your ear, Mr Lawrence, if I may.'

'Say it out, man. If you've got news, we should all hear it.'

'It's for you alone,' Bill Bate said.

Clive Lawrence dismounted and handed his reins to Clem Rose. 'Very well. Keep it short,' he said.

He walked with Bate out of earshot. Bate told him about the death of the priest in plain words.

'A priest from Middlemarsh?' Lawrence said. 'There's no priest at Middlemarsh that I know of. A nobody, therefore. He pointed his gun at you and you killed him in self-defence. When I get back this evening, we'll deal with it. I'll talk to the police.'

'It can't be as simple as that,' Bate said. 'There's a man dead and I killed him. There's a law that's bigger than you or me, Mr Lawrence. It'll have to go before a court.'

'I am the court,' said Clive Lawrence laughing, 'and when I choose, my word is the law.'

'With respect, I don't think so,' replied Bate.

'Do you not?' the squire said in a changed voice. 'Then you may suffer for your ignorance. If you wish me to put this matter before the county court, I shall do so. Consider it done. I have more important things to deal with. We are off to look for the deserter. I want news of him, and of my horses.'

'This hullabaloo is all for the boy?'

'*Hullabaloo*? The ''boy'' is a deserter and a horse thief. The surest way to get him is to go out and look for him myself.'

'Forgive me, Mr Lawrence, but this is not the proper way.'

'Forgive you? I will not. What the devil's got into you? Is my authority not good enough for you all of a sudden? This is ill-timed, Bate, and ill-advised. Tell me where I can find the deserter and my horses and perhaps I can forget this interview.'

'I do not wish you to forget it, sir. Certainly I shall not. I do not know where the lad is and that is the truth. But if I did, I would not tell you.'

'Is that how the land lies, Bill Bate? Hear these tidings then: I shall recommend to the county court that they try you for murder, since this is what you wish. I shall say no word in your defence. If by some chance they should still set you free, now or at a later time, there will be no work for you on my estate, or in the villages where I am known, or in Cerne where a word in a few ears will ensure you an early retirement. I had marked you out as a good man and a good servant, but I was wrong.'

'I think you do not know the difference between the two,' said Bill Bate.

'Clem, bring me my horse,' called the squire turning on his heel.

210

'Here, Jepp! Here, Fleece! Here, Vagabond!' called the Whips. The hunt left heading east towards Hammond, source of the last intelligence about the wanted man. The huntsmen were told to seek information from farmers in their yards and labourers in the fields, and the Whips were ordered to blow their horns, and anyone met on the road was instructed to pass the word. Only Christian Thick said nothing to anybody, but kept his eyes on the soft verges and examined the hoofprints in gateways and dogtrotted to and fro, axe on his shoulder, well aware that such a storm would have washed out everything but the tracks made that very morning.

'We'll raise the countryside, Clem,' the squire said. 'There won't be a tussock in middle Dorset where the boy can sit down without somebody knowing it.' In Buckland, he called a halt outside the church, where people had started to gather for the morning service, for the day was Sunday and the time was close on ten o'clock.

The vicar of Buckland came out of his church vested in his robes and bearing himself with appropriate solemnity.

'I take a dim view of sporting on the sabbath, Squire,' said the cleric. He was an elderly man, with an angular face nearly as grey as his hair, but there was a sharpness in his eye and voice.

'This is no sport, Reverend,' the squire said. 'More of a military manoeuvre. Bring out your parishioners, if you please, for I have a word to say to them.'

'The service is about to begin and there can be no call for its untimely interruption.'

'Saving your grace, Reverend, there are times when the soldiery must take precedence over the ministry.'

'You are referring to the murder of St Thomas à Becket, perhaps?'

'If you will not call them out, then I shall come in,' said Colonel Lawrence, dismounting.

'Then it is of the Puritan Levellers let loose by Oliver Cromwell that you are thinking. We have a sacred order in our church, Mr Lawrence. The bells are rung. The congregation gathers. The priest approaches the altar and the rite of worship begins. The precedence of the soldiery over the ministry heralds disorder and damnation.'

'It is you that shall be damned if you stand in my way,' Lawrence said. He marched towards the door of the church, and the elderly vicar took a step back.

Inside the church were a score of yeoman farmers and cottagers with their wives and children, all in dark Sunday suits and sombre Sunday gowns. In the front pews were ranged the important families of the neighbour hood, including a fat man with a scarlet face and no visible neck, who had two hundred acres between Buckland and Melcombe and who was known to walk no further than the apple orchard at the back of his house. He heaved himself up from his pew and met the colonel in the aisle.

'Welcome, Lawrence,' he said. 'Why the fancy dress?'

But the colonel pushed past him and marched to the front of the nave, pausing only an instant before climbing the few steps to the pulpit. At the back of the church a few of the huntsmen had come in. The vicar, in protest, had remained at the west door.

It was the first time that the squire of Minterne had found himself in a pulpit looking down on the upturned faces of the faithful and it called forth a high sense of righteousness which was new in him.

'The fugitive who is lurking somewhere within a few miles of this holy place,' he said, 'is the embodiment of unredeemed man. The man who will not fight for his country in its hour of need is a pariah among good Christian people, a standard-bearer for Satan.'

The congregation was puzzled. Some thought that pariah was a kind of dog and were not certain how a dog might be a standard-bearer. But those few steps that lift the pulpit above the nave lift the pulpiteer beyond the commonplace.

'He has sinned not against the flesh but against the spirit, and it is the sword of the spirit that we must raise against him,' declared the squire ... and so on, spiralling upward to where heaven is guarded by archangels armed with spears of gold.

There were a few in the congregation that day who felt themselves inspired by the squire's vaulting sermon, or daunted by his authority, and when the hunt continued on its way some time later, the ranks of foot soldiers had swollen. But the majority were relieved when the squire was replaced by their sensible vicar, who preached them a very different kind of sermon about the dangers of muddling the effable with the ineffable. Ineffable was in the hymns. They didn't know effable for certain, but he told them that a man who didn't want to fight was an effable matter and the sword of the spirit was not. The general feeling after the service was over was that the young chap ought to be allowed to go home.

The landowner with the red-moon face made his excuses. 'Good show, Lawrence, and all that, but I'm afraid my leg's been playing up ... Not the right day for an outing. Sunday too. Bit of a palaver, isn't it? One young fellow. Better leave him to the police, what?'

'If your leg's crocked, by all means go back for your dinner,' said Lawrence shortly.

The hunt took the Hammond road out of Buckland, climbing by the tiny hamlets of Rew and Charnell and Brockhampton and seeking news there. At Brockhampton Green, they heard that a party of three people with horses, one of the horses ridden by a girl, had passed by in the rain the previous afternoon, coming from Hammond and heading for Duntish. The hunt followed the Duntish road.

By Bewley Wood, a motorcycle appeared on the road behind them, furiously driven by a man in the uniform of an army captain. The last of the riders turned at the approaching noise, and some of the hounds started barking, as Charles Yeoman drove right among them, twisting the machine this way and that, using his feet to turn and keep steady. One of the riders called out in protest 'Look out, man!', but Charles opened the throttle and drove on through the pack, overtaking at last the colonel of militia and master of foxhounds and proprietor of the most desirable property in middle Dorset.

'Stop your engine, sir!' Mr Lawrence said, but Charles ignored him.

'I demand to know what is the purpose of this,' Charles shouted.

Mr Lawrence did not care for demands. 'Our quarry is a deserter and horse thief,' he said. 'You failed to bring back my horses or to apprehend your brother. The police have apparently done nothing, so I have taken the matter into my own hands.'

'Then you are a blackguard, sir, and I say so loudly in front of these gentlemen. I appeal to them to give up this outrageous business and go back to their homes. The matter will be taken care of by the army, which needs no help from a mob with horns and dogs.'

'Stand aside, sir, and allow us to do our duty as Englishmen,' the squire said.

'I will not stand aside,' Charles Yeoman said.

He sat astride his motorcycle with the motor idling, barring the way down the narrow road, one man on a machine against half-a-dozen horsemen and a pack of dogs. It was the machine that infuriated them, the vanguard of an unacceptable future. Clive Lawrence dug his spurs into his horse's flanks and the animal leapt forward. Charles opened the throttle wide, applying and releasing the clutch, but the squire kept coming, lifted his riding crop and brought it down savagely across his back. It was the signal for the rest of them to advance. Clem Rose struck Charles across the face with his whip, and the others closed in around him.

At the first blow Charles ducked. At the second, he raised one arm over his head. The third threw him from the saddle. The clutch was released with the throttle stuck open and the motorcycle careered into the pack of hounds. One of them was caught squarely by the front wheel, carried yelping across the verge and crushed against the hedge, where it was skewered by a sharp stick and died at once.

The riders dismounted. Two of them picked up the dead hound called Mascot and laid it over the back of one of the horses. Clem Rose set about the motorcycle, stamping on the headlight to shatter the glass, ripping out the plug leads and flinging them over the hedge. They mounted and rode on quickly, without looking back. Charles lay on the road with his hands covering his head and blood on his neck.

The foxhounds were in a state of puzzlement. Out at last with horses and huntsmen and horns, they had been forbidden to follow the scent

215

of fox. The woods and the fields were banned to them. The hunt crawled from place to place, stopping and starting. If the dogs found a scent, they were called back and cursed; if they got excited they were rounded up and yelled at. They had stood bewildered as their men attacked another man, a machine exploded from a scrum and one of their number died yelping in the hedge. Blood dripped from the corpse of the hound flung across the horse's back. Blood was on the road. Blood was up.

The hunt rode on through the middle-Dorset lanes. The rumour of the hunt and its purpose had spread among the villages. In Duntish they knew of its coming before they heard the hounds and the horns. Men coming from church went out to see what was what and some of them stayed to see what would be.

At *The Duntish Rings*, Cockler's dog was the first to register the hunt's approach. He stood in the yard and barked until Cockler came out. 'So the hounds are out on a Sunday,' Cockler said to his dog. 'What would you make of that, my friend? Out for a sniff of the morning breezes, do you reckon? No? Coming this way? Very likely. Now what might they be after, do you think?'

He stepped back to the open door of the taproom and called out.

'Mrs D! You'd best step out here a minute.'

The landlady joined him at the door.

'See here, Mrs D. There's hounds and riders coming this way, which might mean trouble for us. You can leave this part to me, if you like. If there's a spot of fibbing to be done, my memory's what you might call selective, and I may not altogether recollect who was 'ere last night and where they might be now.'

'Just as you please, Mr Cockler,' she said, and went back inside.

When the riders and the hounds began funnelling through the gateway and into the yard, Cockler let them mill around for a minute or two while he got a look at how many they were and who was in charge before stepping up to the figure of Clive Lawrence with his colonel's cap and veteran's sword.

'Are you the publican?' Clive Lawrence said.

'Publican and sinner at your service, my lord,' said Cockler. 'Ostler, barman and bottle washer.'

'We are looking for a man who was here last night.'

'Then I hope for my sake it ain't me,' Cockler said.

'There were men staying here. A man in uniform with a motorcycle. His brother, too, I suspect.'

'In addition to myself,' said Cockler, 'there were three men here last night. Each of them has departed. Separately and in different directions.'

'We're after a young man, tall, with black hair.'

'There was one such. He left very early, on horseback.'

'And where did he go?'

Cockler said that this was unknown to him. He had not thought to demand itineraries or explanations, he said, it being beyond the scope of his curiosity or responsibility. 'You see, Colonel,' he said, 'this here is an inn and neither a police station nor a customs post. Therefore travellers are free to come and go as they please, without giving their names or purposes, which is I believe the procedure in any civilised country such as France and Russia and the other warring nations, although I do not include Germany of course.'

'Are you trifling with me, sir?'

'Perish the thought!' Cockler said. 'I am sure that your reasons for wishing to get hold of this young feller are powerful ones. I wish I could march into those bushes over there and haul 'im out for you. However, the fact is that he still enjoys the freedom of the park, if we might put it that way, so not even decent citizens like myself could rightly lay a hand on 'is shoulder and say: stop where you are, friend, until 'is lordship gets here. You get my meaning, I expect.'

'You haven't been long in these parts, have you my man? Do not make the mistake of irritating me. You may find it uncomfortable. Clem,' he said, turning to the huntsman at his shoulder, 'have a look in the stables to see what horses are there.'

'Very good, Mr Lawrence,' answered Clem Rose.

'Don't bother threatening me, my lord,' said Cockler. 'I've not been comfortable since the moment you set foot on the place. Half-a-dozen horses and a pack of dogs arriving unexpectedly is not a common sort of business, and searching a person's stables without asking is not a common sort of behaviour. If you'd asked, I could've told you there was one old carthorse in the stables, and if you'd opened the door and stood aside, I could've whistled her out for you to 'ave a look at.'

'I prefer to conduct my own search,' the squire said.

'So you do, my lord. And nobody in 'is right mind would think to stand in your way, least of all myself. But if you want my advice, what you want to do is to wait around and have a word with the young feller's brother, an army man like yourself. A major in fact, with battledress and badges to prove it.'

'I have already met with Captain Yeoman.'

218

'Captain is it? I miscounted a pip and caused a promotion. Never mind. If you have spoken with the gen'leman in question, you will 'ave learned that 'is brother is due back with 'is regiment in France. Tomorrow at the latest. Necessities of war, you see. You and I might fancy a nice morning of viewhalloo and the bark of frightened foxes, but there's others with regimental orders in their pockets.'

'Foxes have got nothing to do with it.'

'Quite right, my lord. With a fox in yer chicken run and a gun on yer arm, you may be tempted to give 'im a blast for the sake of the fowl. But when yer fox is quietly feeding 'is family with rabbits and the odd duck, 'e can safely be left to get on with 'is own life. If the hounds are out for a run and a bit of a laugh, I'm right with you m'lord. In fact the idea's just come to me that I may as well have a break from my duties as barman and bottle washer, hop on the old nag and ride out to keep yer company.'

'I have no wish for your company,' the squire returned curtly. 'If I had the time, however, I might inquire into your own reasons for washing bottles at a public house instead of putting on a uniform and doing your bit for your country.'

'To tell the truth, sir, it wasn't so much corporals that we was short of on the front line as colonels. Every trench had a corporal or two standing by, but colonels was in such short supply that they kept them well out of the way, looking after the grand scheme of things at the back. It's a special sort of chap as makes the rank of colonel, see, so it's only natural that they 'ave to keep 'em where they can bend over their maps without 'aving to watch their behinds. And it's my guess that they keep the pick of the bunch to look after the home front, where there's hounds that need exercise and young chaps late in getting back to their regiments where they belong. It'd be a rare pleasure for me to tag along and get a ringside view of 'ow these important matters are conducted by someone so important as yerself.'

Clive Lawrence looked the man up and down with a look that had it been a blade might have sliced him in two.

'Very well,' he said. 'Come along with us if you can keep up. You know the deserter by sight, which we do not. Clem, keep an eye on this chap and when the hunting's over remind me that I'm not quite through my conversation with the publican who lectures on the duties of colonels. The problem now, gentlemen, is which way from here.'

This difficulty was solved by the appearance of Christian Thick, who entered the yard by the stone archway issuing a warbling cry of unusual pitch and volume which commanded the attention of everybody there.

'Christian has summat to get off his chest,' Clem Rose said. 'Step up Christian, lad, and let us know what's on your mind.'

In response Christian took hold of Clem Rose's reins with the hand that wasn't holding his axe and tugged him towards the big meadow that lay on the north side of *The Duntish Rings*.

'Let the reins go, Christian. I'll be right behind you,' Clem said.

In a few minutes Clem was back.

'Christian 'ave come on the tracks of horses, Mr Lawrence. Crossing the big piece o' plough out that way,' he said, pointing. 'There was three of them, 'e made me to understand, two of them being your very own. I get the feeling that Christian do know the third animal, too. 'E stayed to study the prints.'

'Publican!' Lawrence called out.

Cockler emerged from the barn leading his heavy horse and tied its halter rope round its neck as reins.

'At your service, your lordship,' he said.

'Who is riding my horses?'

'A skinny one and a square one? A credit to your stables, sir.'

'Who is riding them I want to know.'

'The lad and his sister. Taking them back to where they came from, as I understand.'

'There's a third horse. Whose horse is that?'

'You don't need to be bothering with that one, my lord. A man came through this morning. Took some refreshment and went on.'

'Very well. Publican, see to it that the dead hound gets a decent burial when you return.'

'Right you are, my lord. It shall go down with military honours and the flag at half mast as if it were a foot soldier on the Somme.'

The body of the hound was taken from where it lay over the horse's rump and laid by the wall of the barn. The Whips began moving out from the yard, calling the dogs. 'Come in Jepp! Come Fleece! Come, Vagabond!' Cockler sprung smartly on to his carthorse's bare back and rode off with the hunt. His woolly dog remained in the stables where it had been recommended to stay put until further notice.

Chapter Fourteen

Hullabaloo

how do you like your blue-eyed boy mister death (ee cummings)

CLOSER to red indian than gypsy, closer to the earth than the sky, closer to the world of animals than to the thoughts of men, Christian Thick was wholly engaged with the three sets of hoofprints. The ground was still very wet, untrodden that morning by all save the occasional bird and travelling hare. Each set of hoofprints was quite different to his eye, in size and detail. The bay mare with one nail loose on the rear left shoe. The young black filly, narrow hooves, almost dainty. The heavy prints of the piebald, which well he knew from the marsh. The girl must be on the filly, and the deeper impression of the mare's hooves showed that it carried a heavier rider, the man they called the deserter, he supposed. On the stallion, the stallion's owner, naturally, who kept Christian in servitude.

He had no defence against the tyranny of the priest. No words with which to object, no higher authority to appeal to. He had only what set him apart, the skills of a man born to live and die under the treetops. These remarkable skills were of little interest to the priest, who regarded them, as most folk did, as a primitive aberration. Christian lived on Urley Moor not for the sake of the scant meals that the priest allowed him but for a warm bed of straw in a stable where no one ever came, for the isolation of the priest's solitary ways, for the pleasure of gathering plants or bark or fungi. Above all for the marsh itself, mislaid and forgotten by the dry land, sunk in its melancholy mood.

For the marsh with its rich willows flinging in a westerly wind and the surface of its pools jumping and shivering in the hard rain. For this Christian endured the priest's unrelenting disdain. The man would never strike him; the axe was on hand to see to that. But how he liked to hound him with contemptuous words and harry him with scathing looks and order him to servile tasks, watching for the hint of defiance which would mean no meal that day.

Now Christian tracked his master. No one had told him why, but he had his own version of that. With the priest rode the girl with skin soft as rabbit fur, smoother than birchbark. The girl in whom he had sensed the presence of some sweet secret. He wanted to learn what unknown feeling shone in that depth, like the eyes of a fledgling in the dark of a treecreeper's hole. *She* was riding with *him* and surely not by choice. The filly was not roped to the piebald, for the prints went away from each other, sometimes far away, before coming back together again. But the priest would have his gun, as he always did.

So much irritating bustle for a tracking that was simple in the wet. Hullabaloo, he had heard Bill Bate say, a word he didn't know, and the word came to describe this thing he couldn't grasp, this hunt without foxes, these bugles vainly bugling, this slow circling among tiny hamlets, and the killing of the dumb hound under the wheel of a machine. There was nothing plainer than the prints across the plough, along the lanes, over meadows, but the hullabaloo was behind. *Hullabaloo, hullabaloo,* echoed in Christian's head.

A stranger had joined them at the Duntish inn, a blow-in, chirpy like a sparrow. This one called Cockler went bareback on a horse built for work. Christian admired it. If you need a horse, pick the strongest. If you must ride, ride without clutter. Offered a seat behind Cockler, Christian took it, for his legs were tiring. 'Come on up, Christy lad,' Cockler went. 'Room for two and more.' Christian worried for his axe, but Cockler laid it with the handle underneath him and the blade lying flat on the horse's rump.

'Christy'. A new name that tasted good. The man held him when he needed to lean down. Talked to him while they rode, with Christian scanning the ground. 'Nobody can track them like you, Christy lad,' said Cockler's voice in his ear. 'They'd lose the trail in a jiff. Got you to do the work, Christy, while they play hunters ... '

The words were sweetly said, but there was more to come, hard for Christian to follow over the uneven ground of thought. Deserters and tribunals. *Hullabaloo*.

They rode by the fields between Duntish and Buckland with the hounds floundering in the mud and the horses bogging in the slush. But not Cockler's carthorse, who stolidly planted her big feet and stolidly drew them forth. Behind her, the huntsmen cursed and the paler colours of the hounds turned all dirt brown.

They came at last to the road at Buckland, where some of the hunters had come through earlier that morning leaving a confusion of prints. Christian slipped down from the carthorse and got to his knees to examine them, and when he found the prints of the big piebald and the bay mare with the loose shoe, they led down the path towards the village in the company of tracks of other horses, and so he missed the departure of the girl and her filly, who had gone up the road instead. Later the prints of the piebald and the bay mare climbed away from the village, but as they left the valley land, the tracks grew fainter over the short chalk-grown grass. There were only the slightest signs, sometimes just an edge written against a tussock or grass stems bent back. That there was no trace of the filly's hoofprints did not surprise him, for she was a small horse lightly mounted and there was no mud to tell the tale. Once there had been nothing at all for a spell and Christian thought he should go back, but then there was a pile of droppings, cold but not old. They were the piebald's, he knew. Climbing the northern face of Giant Hill, he was anxious for his axe. He turned to see if it might slip from under Cockler's seat. Cockler grinned, patting the handle.

From the far end of the ridge above them rose a spiral of smoke. Christian saw it while it was still no more than a thread hung in the sky and before the other riders he knew the place where the fire was lit. When he spotted a black-and-white dog on the skyline, anxiety began to swell inside him. He twisted round to lay hands on his axe.

'There'll be no need for that, Christy lad,' Cockler said, but Christian elbowed him aside and grabbed hold of the familiar handle, worn smooth by the years between his hands.

The hounds knew the black-and-white dog as not of their tribe. Boldly marked, ground-hugging, vulpine. They bayed as they breasted the ridge, with a quarry to chase at last. Cockler's big horse laboured on the steep slope.

'Keep 'em steady, Squire. We don't want to trip up at the last, do we?' Cockler called out. 'The hounds 'ave gone after a dog, that's all.' But Lawrence was on his own acres now, belligerent, impatient to press on. Muttering, he told Clem Rose to call the riders to order and slowly they fell in line behind the carthorse, deferring to their demon scout.

The chalk-cut Giant of Cerne lay to the south, still concealed by the ridge. The smoke of the fire was visible but not its source. The old cart-horse was at a standstill by the time she reached the top and the other riders milled around her, eyeing the hounds, which were streaming down the westerly slope in pursuit of the black-and-white dog.

His patience used up, Lawrence spurred his horse after the hounds. 'Every man for himself,' he shouted, 'and the devil take the hindmost.'

Hindmost came Cockler, Christian and the carthorse. The lie of the land was unknown to Cockler and the only Giant he knew of was a seven-footer from Barking who had to stoop to get in at the door of *The Dog*. He had a look where the ribbon of smoke was and he had a look where the hounds were headed, with Lawrence and the other huntsmen spurring their horses down the slope after them.

'What do you think, Christy?' Cockler said. 'We could take a ride along the top and see what that fire's about, and if we have to go down afterwards, we can do it, but damned if I fancy going down there and having to come back up again.'

He urged his horse along the top of the ridge. Below them, they saw John French dodging and doubling to keep ahead of the hounds. 'Go on, my lovely. Oats and bran mash,' Cockler said, bending his head to the horse's ear. She never knew a stick or a whip, Cockler's mare, and perhaps she knew the words instead. She went on at a canter, bringing the hindmost first to the scene on the trendle.

By a blazing fire stood a girl and a man with a gun over his arm. Tethered to a stunted thorn tree beyond them were the squire's two horses. The girl held some articles on the palm of her outstretched hand, apparently offering them to the man beside her. The man reached out, took the objects from the girl and put them in his pocket, lifting his gun in the direction of the newcomers.

The priest eyed the riders. Christian Thick looked down at his axe, running his thumb along the edge of the blade. Cockler watched the girl, measuring the distance to her over the grass. The cries of the hounds grew louder from below. Then over the horizon of grass appeared the black-and-white collie called John French.

Sir John French. Let him have his full title, for he had earned it. Lost his master at Hammond, tracked the piebald horse to Duntish. False scents and inexplicable events. Found him and lost him again. In the morning found him once more and tracked him to the Giant at a distance. When had the dog slept, when eaten? He had lain up on Giant Hill, watching his master with the girl by the fire. Pricked up his ears at every gesture made by the priest. Half-rose from the grass when the voices were raised, remaining like that until his legs shook. When the sound of the hunt had come to his ears, he had made off along the ridge and found a place to watch the hunt climbing the slope, crouching low to the ground, spying between stems of grass.

Is a dog aware of its own colour? Had his coat been grey or a shade of brown, he might have lain unseen in the grass like a stone. But the flashes of white on black signalled to the eyes of the hounds and they came after him. He fled away from them down the western slope, looking for cover. But there was none and the hounds gained on him, with their long legs and the pent-up energy of the pack. He took them nearly to the bottom of the hill, darting and twisting. Only when he knew they must catch him did he make his last mad dash back up to where his master stood.

The trendle was bordered by a raised bank. Beyond the bank stood the priest and the girl and beyond them Jack's great bonfire. French came to the bank, the hounds snarling and snapping at his heels. For an instant they slowed as they caught sight of the people, the horses and the flames of the fire, and in this instant French launched himself straight at his master, as if to land in his very arms. The man lifted his gun high in the air to get it out of the way and took a step back. The dog's body hit him on the chest and he stumbled backwards under its momentum, struggling to stay on his feet. The heat from the fire scorched his back and his neck. Now the dog saved itself, twisting and leaping away from where he clung to his master's body, pitching the so-called priest of Urley House into the flames of the fire of Samhain.

The girl screamed. The hounds swarmed around her and she fell to her knees, covering her head with her hands. John French was buried under a furious scrum of hounds.

For centuries, this hilltop site had lain silently above the valleys, above the trees and streams and houses, disturbed by nothing more violent than strong winds, nothing more noisy than the cropping of sheep on the turf. Now it was as if some dreadful power was roused amid the burning and the screaming and the yelping of the dogs. As if the wargod had awoken from his long sleep demanding blood.

Cockler slid from his horse, strode forward amongst the hounds, picked up the girl and bore her away. Christian Thick stood by the fire with his axe raised over the body of the burning man that seethed and crackled in the awful flames. The heat drove off the hounds and John French limped away but Christian stood on by the fire, his axe still lifted high above his head, retreating at last as the heat singed his clothes.

The body was black by the time the huntsmen dragged it from the fire. You couldn't see what it had been wearing, or anything of its features. They had to let it cool down before they could load it on to a horse and take it down the hill to Cerne, and on the morrow the burial took place in a west wind fit to unroof the abbey. Dust to dust, ashes to ashes, said the minister. 'Amen' they answered back.

There was no name on the tombstone they raised later, only three words: Rest in Peace. Lawrence saw it for himself and said the family had been right not to commemorate a deserter and a coward. He'd heard the rumours: it was another body in the coffin or, as some asserted, the sexton had found nothing but burned clothes when he came to shift the man's remains into their box. But Lawrence had seen the man pulled from the fire and ridden down the hill by the side of the blackened corpse and he set no store by local gossip.

Two months later, on 1 January 1917, Maggie Fox married Charles Yeoman in the church at Hammond in a quiet ceremony attended by Grammer Score and her sister, and Bill Bate of Cerne. Cockler was there too, with Mrs M. Cockler (so it said on the sign above the door of *The Duntish Rings*). Bate told Cockler that he was employed at Milton Abbey to restore the stonework of the church. It would take him many years, he said, and indeed it was to take him a lifetime.

Maggie carried in her purse the pages torn from a notebook on which was written the last letter Jack Yeoman wrote from France and by Louis's grave she read it once again.

Dear Charles and Dearest Maggie,

There's a fellow going on leave today who will take this for me, to avoid the censors. I want you to know that you were right – both of you were right – when you urged me to return to the front. The war is an insanity, but when I tried to leave I took it with me. The violence came back with me and spread like a contagion. The battle came with me, and the infernal guns. I could not escape them by running away.

After leaving you at the Giant, Maggie, I rode to Dorchester, setting the horse loose outside the town. At the barracks, I told them I must have lost my memory because when I woke up and knew who I was, two weeks had gone by and I was in Dorset instead of with my regiment in France. The captain who saw me said that I would be sent to a military hospital. He warned me that they would have further questions for me there. I said that I didn't need a hospital, I needed a ship to France. I could see that he didn't believe me about the amnesia, but he liked it when I said that about the ship. There were regulations and procedures, he said, but I thought I could convince him because he wanted to be convinced. He was an old man, too old to fight I suppose, and I felt a sudden sympathy for him, fighting a war from a desk. To hell with the regulations, I said, my fellows are dying in the trenches and I want to be there with them. Where's your uniform, he said. Damned if I know, I said. Give me a uniform with a stripe on the sleeve and a pass with a stamp on it and I can do the rest. I walked out of there the next morning with a lance-corporal's uniform and a medical certificate and a letter to my company captain. The war is an insanity but it does not make us all insane. Here we clean our rifles and scour the pots and scrub the blood from our battledress. We pass round the photographs of our people at home although we rarely speak of the old days, before the war. We are not who we were. I am not who I was. I am become insignificant like a dot on a map, a name on an endless register, a minuscule bug in a crumbling tree.

I have not learned to kill. But now I am back, I feel we are on the same side again. I didn't realise I would feel something like that, but perhaps it is what I came for. You and me, and the men on the farm and Bill Bate and the rest of them at home and Cockler too, bless his laughing eyes.

In our company, the lieutenants and the captain are respected. Some of them are very brave men. We despise the visiting redtabs and we are suspicious of majors and colonels. The brigadiers and generals we assume to be ignorant and we cannot forgive them for that. We do not believe that there is a plan to win this war, or even that it can be won. But we believe it will be over one day, when no one is left standing or there is no more metal to melt down for the shells or someone sticks a knife through the Kaiser. One day, at any rate, and we pray for it.

I send my best love to you both, and if the worst should happen, you will look after each other, I know.

Your loving brother,

Jack.

The letter was dated 2 December 1916. Jack was killed in action a few days later, not far from the hill the French troops called Mont-maudit, whence the battlefront had not moved.

On a warm evening in the spring of the following year, Margaret Yeoman sat with Marguerita Cockler outside *The Duntish Rings*. Cockler was off with his dog hunting up a couple of rabbits for supper, Marguerita said.

As they sat talking, the big gate to the yard swung open and Christian Thick entered from the road, with the piebald stallion walking behind him. He came up with a slight bow and stood before them. His clothes were neater and his boots were stouter. Whatever their surprise at this unexpected visit, the women invited him to join them for a cup of tea, and he sat with them. When he had finished his tea, he held out his hand to Maggie Fox with the red and white dice, somewhat charred, lying on his palm. Cross Six was the sign they showed, but Christian took no notice of it. He offered them to her and she accepted them and he got up to go.

'Thank you, Christian,' she said.

He nodded and smiled. There were not many people in Buckland or Minterne or Middlemarsh who had seen Christian smile, and it was a goodly sight.

'Christian, did you ever see the priest's dog again?' Marguerita asked him.

He shook his head and continued shaking it, as one would say: no, no, no, not him, not that one. Then he went, turning at the gate and raising his hand beside his face in farewell. The stallion, which had neither halter nor rope, followed him from the yard.

Maggie Yeoman had learned much from Marguerita about the sources and courses of illness and the virtues of plants, but Marguerita insisted she was no teacher. 'I am a *friend*,' she said. The word from her lips sounded weighty and enduring as if it meant more than is common. They had rarely spoken of the dice, or the ex-priest of Urley Moor or the events at the inn on the eve of All Hallows. The dice might have gone into the coffin with the priest, Maggie had thought, and on the whole she reckoned it a fit place for them.

'Cockler drove me over to Cerne a little while back,' Marguerita said when Christian had gone. 'I happened on Bill Bate in the street and we had a talk. I asked him whether he'd seen the dog in Cerne. There weren't no stray sheepdogs in Cerne, he said.

'The hounds didn't kill the dog at the Giant, even though you told me he was set on by the whole pack. The dog is looking for his master, Maggie, and will go on looking until kingdom come.

'The priest was never a priest, not in Middlemarsh nor anywhere else. He wore the cleric's collar to mask his designs. You know how it is, Maggie, when people see the collar. Don't ask me what those designs were. Where there are secrets there is always mischief. Where there is power, there are always thralls to power. Human flotsam is what he was. Gytrash. Ask in Middlemarsh and Holnest. Ask who knows about the priest's past or his parents. The so-called priest did not come from these parts or from this bank and shoal of time, and nor did the dog called John French.'